THE RUSSIAN BILLIONAIRE

GEORGIA LE CARRE

ACKNOWLEDGMENTS

Much love and many thanks to:

Elizabeth Burns
Nichola Rhead
Brittany Urbaniak
Tracy Gray

978-1-913990-18-3

KONSTANTIN

https://www.youtube.com/watch?v=Lgs9QUtWc3M

My cell phone vibrates gently on my office desk. I glance at it. Stephan Priory. As I reach for the phone the girl under the desk stops sucking my cock and stares at me with her thickly lashed baby blue eyes.

"Don't stop," I instruct, as I hit the accept option.

Obediently, she continues bobbing her head up and down, her voluptuous red lips making wet sounds. She's very good at this. Years of experience, no doubt.

"Stephan," I say crisply into the phone, as I watch her big red mouth swallow my cock. I have a thing for girls with naturally big lips.

"Good evening, Mr. Tsarnov. Sorry to disturb you, but I just wanted to give you a heads up on a... um, " he clears his throat, "developing situation. I'm afraid we're going to have a slight PR problem when the Anton scandal breaks next month."

My voice is cold and forbidding. "Why? What does that fool have to do with me?"

"Well, you know what the... er... political climate is in Washington these days if you're a Russian billionaire. Pure paranoia and guilt by association."

"I met him *once* at a party," I growl, irritated.

"I know, I know, but unfortunately, there's a photo circulating online of you and him at that party."

I rake my fingers through the girl's long silky hair, and she moans softly. "So?"

"The problem is I've been informed by my contact at the Washington Post that they're planning to run with a center page spread story of the situation, and they're going to use that photo, but crop it to seem as if you are entertaining him alone on your yacht."

The girl starts to bob faster, as I watch my glistening cock slide in and out of her mouth. I weigh my options. Take the trouble to kill the story. Nah, those self-righteous pricks at the Washington Post can go and fuck themselves. "Let them run their lies. I have survived worse. Anything else?"

"Yeah." He clears his throat. "I'm afraid there'll be pics of you and Putin looking very chummy too."

"For fucks sake," I explode.

The girl stops and looks at me questioningly.

"Carry on," I rasp at her.

"Sorry?" Stephan asks.

"I'm not talking to you," I mutter.

"Oh!" He pauses, then continues. "We need to do something about this. The Hansom Cross contract is up for grabs in two months, and they won't want to be tarnished by this mess. At least not if it's going to be portrayed the way the Washington Post is planning to print it."

I close my eyes and luxuriate in the hot, wet mouth of the girl. "You obviously have a suggestion."

"Yes, yes, as a matter of fact I do," he says eagerly." We should mount our own PR offensive before they run their grubby story. A distraction is the answer. You should do something big and flashy. Something that gets you in the media and makes you get noticed for all the right reasons."

"Mmmm..."

"I'm thinking about the Huntingdon Children's Hospital Charity dinner gala. You're attending it on the 25th of this month. One of the things they'll be auctioning off is dinner dates. I suggest you blow half a million on one of the girls at the auction. A bit of philanthropy never did any harm, especially if it's also sexy enough to make it into lots of the newspapers, maybe even the evening news on some TV stations. I can almost see the headlines. Billionaire Russian throws a half a million on dinner date for children's charity."

"Who are these girls?" I ask, watching her cheeks hollow, as my glistening dick flows out of her red mouth.

"I'm not a hundred percent sure, but I think they're agency girls."

"Prostitutes?"

"Of course not," Stephan cries, alarmed as only an Englishman can be.

The girl feels my dick grow larger and starts sucking harder.

"The women at these events are usually society ladies, or aspiring actresses and girls wanting to earn a bit of extra money. In this case, I believe the hospital is using an agency. They'll all be really good looking though. Just pick the girl you think will bore you the least. It'll only be a couple hours of your time, but the resulting publicity will be worth it."

"Fine," I reply, cut the line, tossing my phone back on the desk and give my full attention back to the girl under the desk.

.

RAINE

https://www.youtube.com/watch?v=ETxmCCsMoDo

"Oh, Raine, I'm so sorry to hear that. That's terrible. What are you going to do?" Lois, my best friend asks, her forehead creased in a deep frown.

I drop my head in my hands. "I don't know. I feel so damn helpless. Ever since Dad died, things have just been going from bad to worse. Mom's working three jobs, I'm working two, and still there's nothing ever left to put aside for Maddy. If we don't get her the treatment soon... something bad is going to happen."

"Look, I have some money put aside. Take it for her."

"You have a $120,000 put aside?" I joke, but it comes out sounding miserable. My heart is filled with a great bitterness, which keeps me angry and confused inside. More and more I see the world as an unfair place where undeserving fat cats in suits are given government handouts of trillions that they then immediately use to gamble on the stock markets, while ordinary, hard working people like Mom and me are taxed so heavily we can hardly even survive.

"God," Lois breathes. "$120,000."

"And that's just for the operation," I mutter.

"There's got to be something we can do."

I lift my head and look at her. "There is. I'm thinking of working in a strip club."

Her eyes bulge with shock. "What?"

"I know I'm not beautiful in the classic sense of the word, my mouth is too big, but a lot of guys tell me I have a sexy body and that's the important thing in those dark places, isn't it?"

"You're kidding, right?" Lois erupts incredulously.

"Drastic situations call for drastic measures. Anyway, it'll be just for a while. Just until we have saved up enough for Maddy's operation and paid off our old debts."

"No, that is a crazy idea. Do you know how dangerous those strip clubs are? That's where serial killers pick off their prey. And there's drugs there, and the men who—"

"Lois," someone calls from inside the kitchen.

"Coming," Lois shouts over her shoulder, then turns back to me. "I've got to go, but don't do anything stupid. We have to talk about this. Let me see if I can get a loan from the bank or something. We'll find a way out of this problem, okay?"

I sigh. There is no bank in the world who is going to give Lois the kind of money I need. I force a smile. "Okay, let's talk about this another time. I should go home now, anyway. I've got a ton of washing and ironing to do."

Lois's boss pops her head around the back door where Lois and I are standing. "Lois," she says, then stops when she sees me. "Hey, it's Raine, right?"

I nod. "Yeah."

She jerks her head towards the interior of the Lake club. "Go on in, Lois. I want a word with Raine."

Lois widens her eyes at me, then scampers through the kitchen door and disappears around a shelf full of pans.

"What are you doing tonight?" her boss asks me.

I grimace. "It's my night off, so I'm going home to get on with some housework."

She glances at her watch, "Hmmm... You've done bar work before, haven't you?"

I nod. "Yeah."

"Good. I think one of my bartenders is going to let me down. Want to work a shift for me? I'll give you twenty dollars an hour since it's such short notice. It'll be about five hours of work. Cash in hand."

Cash in hand. What's there to even think about? I nod quickly. "Yeah, twenty an hour would be fine."

"Come in then. Let's see if we can find you a white shirt and vest. You can keep the skirt you have on."

Ten minutes later, I'm standing behind the bar, in a crisp white shirt and a maroon vest, watching the great and good come pouring into the party.

"Two martinis, one dry, one dirty, please," a man calls from one end of the bar.

"Coming up," I say and get to work.

An hour passes quickly. Then the guests sit down to dinner and a lull settles around the bar. A woman in a black dress comes to sit at one of the barstools. She must be in her mid-forties. Her hair is colored bright red and she is wearing very fashionable white rimmed glasses. She smiles at me. She orders a frozen margarita with some slices of lemon on the side.

"Why's a girl like you looking so sad?" she asks as I place her drink in front of her.

"I'm not sad," I deny immediately.

"Honey, I know sadness when I see it."

"I'm not sad," I repeat, with a tense smile. A man comes to the bar and orders a beer. I put his beer on a paper coaster in front of him and turn back to the redhead.

"Fine, you're not sad, but let me guess. You have money problems?"

"Who doesn't?" I say lightly.

"I can help you earn some serious money, up to $50,000 and more if it goes well," she drawls, as she picks up one of the thin slices of lemon and licks it like a cat.

RAINE

I keep my face expressionless. "Doing what?"

"There is a gala dinner with a charity auction for the Huntington Hospital on the 25th of this month. One fun part of the auction is for the single male guests. There will be five very rich bachelors that night so there will be five girls up for auction. The men will be bidding for the privilege of buying dinner for the girl of their choice. It's all in good fun, and both the girls and the boys are at the end of the day helping to raise a lot of money for charity." She pauses to take a delicate sip of her drink. "You can be one of those five girls."

I stare at her suspiciously, incredulously. "$50,000 for going on a dinner date?"

"The fifty grand is actually for showing up and taking part. However, if your highest bidder turns out to be the Russian billionaire, Konstantin Tsarnov, who is one of the five bachelor guests, then your ability to earn money grows exponentially."

My jaw drops. Is this woman serious? She sounds like a total fantasist, but she doesn't look like one. She looks very polished and her eyes glitter with intelligence and cunning. Tempted and curious, I decide to play along for a bit.

"Why? What happens if he picks me?"

"Konstantin Tsarnov has something that doesn't belong to him. He stole it from his competitor, who is my client, and my client wants his property back. So, your job will be to persuade him into taking you to his house. Once there you will simply follow the map you will be given, find the thing and exchange it for a... replacement. You don't even have to sleep with him. Invent a believable excuse and leave."

I blink. "I think you want James Bond for this job, not me."

She smiles. "James Bond wouldn't work. The mark likes girls." Her gaze drops to my mouth before coming back up to my eyes. "Girls who look like you. The job is actually much easier than you think. By the time he realizes, if he ever does, the original and you will be long gone."

I touch my mouth self-consciously. "What makes you think he will pick me?"

"To be honest I don't know if he will pick you."

"I see. What happens if he picks one of the other girls then?"

She smiles confidently. "All the other girls have the same deal as you, so it doesn't matter which girl he picks. As far as you're concerned, you'll have dinner at a fancy restaurant with the man who picks you and as soon as you text to tell us it's done, your money will be released from escrow and sent directly into your bank account, making you $50,000 richer."

"What is this thing I am supposed to steal?"

"You wouldn't be stealing," she says quickly. "You would be returning something to its rightful owner. It's a tiny painting of a little boy on a beach. Five inches by six inches, it's small enough to put into your purse, and if you're wondering, its value is purely sentimental. As soon as he chooses you for his dinner companion another $150,000 will be put into escrow. Once you hand the painting over to us, the money will be released to you and you will never hear from us again."

I take a deep breath. Somehow I know she is telling the truth and to be really, really honest I am tempted. She makes it sound like such easy money and we are so desperate for some, but another part of me tells me there is more, much more, that she is not telling me about this job. Five girls at $50,000 each plus another $150,000 makes it $400,000 for a painting that has no value beyond sentimental. I'm not buying it. Something doesn't feel right. I'm not stupid enough to imagine all this money being thrown around is normal. Hell, I can even end up in prison if I get caught. Even the thought of it sends a shiver through my body.

She considers me expressionlessly. "So, what do you say?"

"Thanks for the offer, but no. If your boss wants his property back, he should really find a less underhand way of getting it back."

The woman smiles pleasantly as she pushes her calling card towards me. "Call me if you change your mind before the 25th of this month. I have a strong feeling he will go for you and you can solve our little problem and all your big problems in one fell swoop. I might even be open to negotiating the final price."

Then she stands and leaves.

I pick up the luxuriously thick card.

Catherine Moriarty

There is nothing else on that side of the card. I turn it over and there is a phone number. Definitely fishy. The trash is just to the left of me. I should throw it away right now, but something makes me hesitate. Then, I shake my head at my own stupidity and toss it into the trash. How the hell could I even entertain such a dangerous idea? A deal with the devil is not for me.

Lois's boss is approaching so I get on with cleaning some glasses.

The hours pass quickly and by the time I put the key into the door of our apartment, it's late. I take my shoes off and tip toe into the house. Tonight is the only night my mom doesn't have to work late so I do not want to disturb her if she has fallen asleep in front of the TV. She is not asleep on the sofa. As I pass the bathroom I hear sobbing. Fear grips my heart.

"Mom," I call.

Immediately, the sobbing stops. I turn the door handle and go into the bathroom. My mom is slumped on the floor in the dark.

"Don't switch on the light," she whispers brokenly.

I sit on the floor next to her and take her hand in mine. Her hand is like ice. "What's wrong, Mom?" I ask. My heart is thumping with fear.

"The doctor called. They're going to have to bring her surgery forward. She's not doing so good, Raine. She's struggling. My baby is struggling to live."

"We'll figure it out, Mom."

"No, we won't. I didn't tell you, but I lost my shifts at the grocery store last week. They're cutting back. Not that it matters. Those shifts hardly paid for our weekly food bill."

"Mom, I think I've got a way to pay for Maddy's operation," I whisper in the dark.

RAINE

y mom shoots upwards suddenly and hits the light switch. Light floods the room. She stares at me with a strange expression. Her tired eyes transformed. I see fear and anger glittering in them.

"Doing what?" she asks, in a tight, low voice.

I pull out Catherine's calling card from the pocket of my skirt and hand it to her. Something compelled me and I had fished it out of the trash after my shift. Then I tell her quickly about her proposition. She never takes her eyes off me the whole time I am speaking. When I come to a stop she looks at the card, then she raises her eyes and says one word. The word is harsh and full of pain.

"No." Her voice is hard and stern.

I scramble up to my feet. "Why not? It would be easy money."

My mother looks at me incredulously. "Easy money? Are you kidding? There's no such thing. What if you get caught while you're stealing this painting?"

I stay silent.

"You'll go to prison, Raine. That's what will happen. You'll have a prison record for the rest of your life! Finding work with a criminal record of dishonesty will be near impossible. You want to risk that?"

I look her in the eye. "Yes."

"No, I won't let you do it. There is no way I am going to let one of my children sacrifice herself for the other." Mom can barely repress the shiver of horror that runs through her body.

"It's my decision, Mom. I'm an adult now."

She shakes her head, her eyes pleading. "So you're willing to become a thief?"

I swallow hard and tell her the same lie Catherine told me. "It won't be stealing. I'll just be taking back something that he stole and allowing it to go to the rightful owner."

"If you believe that you're not the girl I thought you were," my mother mutters.

I throw my ace card. "So you'd rather watch Maddy die?"

Mom flinches as if I'd hit her.

"Mom, please give me your blessings because I *am* going to do this."

"I can't give you my blessings to go ahead and destroy yourself."

"What other choice do we have?"

My mother drops her face into her hands and I move forward and take her in my arms. I let her sob her poor heart out while I hold onto her tightly and say again and again, "It's going to be okay, Mom. Everything is going to be fine."

When she stops, she pulls away from me and says, "Call that woman. I want to speak to her."

So I call Catherine Moriarty, and put the phone on speaker mode.

"Hello, this is Raine, the bartender you spoke to tonight."

"Hello, how nice to hear from you again," she drawls.

"My mom wants to have a word with you."

"Of course, put her on," she says confidently.

"What happens if my daughter gets caught while she is switching the painting?"

"The billionaire in question cannot afford any negative publicity at the moment. She will be sent away from his apartment in some humiliation, but she will be paid handsomely for that shame."

"What if he calls the police?"

"We have... people in the force who will take care of her."

"What if the billionaire gets violent with her?"

"Mmm... Kostantin Tsarnov has never shown violent tendencies towards women. It is not his style."

My mother takes a deep breath. "Why did he steal the painting from your client if it is of low value?"

"The theft is part of a long-standing feud between two families."

My mother turns to look at me, her expression is one of defeat. She's hoping Catherine will say something that would make it impossible for me to take the job, but she has found nothing. She shakes her head at me sadly and leaves the bathroom quietly.

I pick up the phone. "What do you need me to do next?"

"Can we meet tomorrow?"

"I'm working tomorrow, but I have an hour for lunch."

"Fantastic." Then she smoothly arranges for us to meet at a restaurant close to my workplace and ends the conversation. I stare at the phone for a few seconds, then I go out into the kitchen where my mother is making tea for us.

We sit at the kitchen table and drink our tea together.

"It's going to be okay, Mom."

She just nods, her expression wretched and gloomy.

RAINE

We meet at a French restaurant. Very upmarket. The hostess actually looks down her nose at me when I arrive. Catherine Moriarty is already at the table sipping from her glass of San Pellegrino. She smiles when she sees me. If she had intended to intimidate me, she is going to be disappointed. I have never eaten in such an expensive restaurant, but I know how they work and exactly how the diners behave like I know the back of my hand.

"Good. You are on time. I hate it when people are late," she says, when I arrive at her table.

A waiter materializes out of nowhere and effortlessly pulls out the chair opposite hers. I slip into it and thank him. He nods at me and withdraws. Someone else comes forward to ask if I would like something to drink.

"Martini, no olives," I say.

"Of course," he says with a nod, and leaves.

I turn my attention back to Catherine.

Her eyes are assessing. "I'm glad you said yes. I have a good feeling about you. You're the right physical type, and you are intelligent. If there's one thing I hate, it's stupid girls. There are too many of them in my line of work."

Her phone rings. She picks it up and says, "Yes. Tell Mr. Nikitin everything is set. He has nothing to worry about." Then she looks up at me and with a glitter of satisfaction, adds, "I've found the perfect bait."

A waiter carrying a basket full of all kinds of bread comes by. Catherine shakes her head and waves him away. I point to a seeded bun and he lays it on the small plate on my right with a pair of tongs.

My glass of martini is put in front of me. I pick it up and take a small sip. Catherine is still listening to something the other person on the phone is saying. So I break a piece of bread and begin to butter it. Catherine ends her call, leans back on her chair and stares at me. There is a strange expression on her face.

"What is it?" I ask.

She flashes the first genuine smile I've seen from her. "You know what?"

I play her game. "What?"

"You're perfect for Konstantin Tsarnov."

"Why?"

"Let's just call it an instinct. I've been in this business a long time and I can tell when I have scored. When I've found that one girl that will be perfect for the job."

"What if he doesn't take me to his apartment?"

"Then you will either have to walk away with just $50,000, an amount I have a feeling is not enough for what you need, or you can arrange another date and try again." She shrugs eloquently. "It will be all up to you. No doubt you have googled him and know he is dashingly handsome. You may even want to sleep with him."

Yes, I did google him and he is drop dead gorgeous, but I zoomed in on his eyes and they are shockingly cold. The eyes of a heartless predator. Not a man I would ever consider sleeping with. I am attracted to guys with warm brown eyes, a cheeky grin, and a wicked sense of humor. Konstantin Tsarnov looks like he wouldn't know humor if it hit him with a wet fish. Besides, men like him disgust me. Their greed is endless. No matter how much money they make it is never enough. They just have to keep on piling on more and more money that they will never be able to spend into their accounts. So I have *absolutely* no intention of sleeping with him. Even the thought fills me with revulsion.

A waiter approaches and hands us menus.

She hands the menu back to him. "I'll have the chicken salad."

I hold my menu out to him. "Same, please."

When he walks away I turn back to her. "Tell me what Konstantin Tsarnov likes."

She leans forward. "He likes variety. He likes change. He likes beautiful women who don't make demands on him. I suppose he likes dumb blondes."

Just as I guessed, Konstantin Tsarnov is a male chauvinist pig. "I thought you said I'm perfect because I'm intelligent..."

"It takes intelligence to play dumb when you're not dumb. I wouldn't dream of entrusting this job to a truly dumb girl."

"I see," I murmur.

"He likes fast cars, good food, and travelling to exotic places, so if you have ever gone to far-flung locations you may talk about that."

"I've never left the States," I admit.

"Hmm... nevermind. He rides horses and is an excellent polo player. He's a great swimmer. He enjoys racing and goes to Monaco and Monte Carlo once a year for the Formula One event. He is also a judo black belt holder." She looks at me hopefully.

"I can swim and I used to ride horses back when we lived on a farm in Missouri," I offer up.

"Yes, yes, talk about horses. He loves them. I believe he keeps a stable of prize-winning horses in England."

Over the next hour, I learn that Mr. Tsarnov is extremely intelligent, cannot bear the company of fools, hates to be bored, and passionately dislikes clingy females. He has a massive yacht parked in the Bahamas, homes in England, Monaco, Dubai, and Moscow, and most important he guards his privacy as jealously as a lioness defends her cubs.

As my plate of half-eaten chicken salad is cleared away, Catherine hands me two NDAs. To my surprise, one is for my mom. For the rest of our lives neither of us will ever be able to speak to anyone about anything that happens pertaining to this job.

KONSTANTIN

https://www.youtube.com/watch?v=UrGw_cOgwa8&
ab_channel=ParlophoneRecords

"I see you haven't bid on anything yet, Mr. Tsarnov," notes Mrs. Lynn de Manafort, the richest woman in New York. And I don't mean that bullshit rich list that Forbes publishes. No, she belongs to that secret rich list only insiders and people in the know, know about.

"Still, I can hardly blame you," she continues. "Except for the Basquiat, everything else has been quite tedious."

Tedious? She has no idea how mind-numbingly dull it has been for me. It'll be a great relief when they auction off the dinner dates, and I can finally leave. I turn towards her carefully powdered face politely.

Her pale blue eyes appear to be genuinely friendly, but I know better. Even so, it is always a surprise to meet one of the members of these generational wealth families who like to pretend they were once insanely wealthy, but have since squandered away their riches. The effortless way they hide their immense power and wealth and blend in with the rest of us taxpayers is quite fascinating.

"Perhaps you will bid on the next event, the dinner dates," she says with a charming smile.

"Perhaps," I murmur, and turn my gaze back towards the stage.

Five young women have come onto the stage. They are all beautiful, with sexy mouths, and stripper bodies, the type I find pleasing. In fact, if I didn't know better I'd think they had all been specially picked to appeal to me. Even so, one of them stands out more than the others.

I focus on her. Long blonde hair, eyes: too far to tell exactly, but either blue or gray, deliciously plump lips, full breasts, curving hips, and... legs that go on forever. I am seated at the head table, close enough to the stage to see her hands trembling. She turns them into fists. Her nervousness makes me curious. I let my eyes wander over to the other girls. They do not show any nervousness at all. In fact, two of them meet my gaze head on, and promise me things. I bring my eyes back to the blonde.

The hunter in me has been triggered.

The Emcee starts the bidding. The first girl is called Alicia. To my surprise, her eyes sweep over in my direction before sliding away quickly. How strange. The bidding starts at ten thousand. The men bid on her and the dinner date is sold for eighty thousand dollars. There is good natured clapping and cheering.

The next is a redhead who, who curiously, shoots a quick look at me before giving a little flirtatious wave at the audience. So, every girl except the blonde has made eye contact. How very interesting.

The bidding starts. The three remaining men bid on her. Dinner with her is sold for a hundred thousand. The Emcee is delighted.

"Let's see if we can up the stakes even more, gentlemen. It's all for a good cause," he encourages with a toothy grin. "Next, we have the very lovely, Raine Fillander. Who will take this beauty out to dinner?"

The blonde steps forward. She gives a quick smile and stares forward. The men start bidding. The Emcee takes them up the garden path right up to a hundred and twenty thousand dollars.

"Do I have a hundred and thirty thousand?" he asks hopefully, glancing around at the men.

"One million," I call.

A hush of disbelief falls over the crowd. The blonde turns towards me, in her oval face, her eyes are huge with shock. Then the well-oiled publicity machine that Stephan pays for bursts into life and countless cameras throw their flashes at Raine Fillander.

In the white light that bathes her, I see that her eyes are blue.

Sapphire blue.

RAINE

The flashes from the cameras that suddenly appear out of nowhere disorientate and startle me. I feel myself shrink back from the blast. What is going on? Surely, I can't have heard right. Then I hear the Emcee, who must also have been in shock, announce, "I have one million. Do I hear one million and ten thousand?"

There is a pause. Followed by silence.

"Going once. Going twice. Sold to Mr. Konstantin Tsarnov."

The entire room breaks into applause. I see a woman in a black dress head in the direction of Konstantin Tsarnov to take his details. My mind is blank as I force a smile and turn towards the direction I had been instructed I must head towards after my stint on the stage. The other two girls who went before me stare at me with a mixture of surprise and hostility.

"Do you know him?" one of them demands.

I shake my head in a daze. In my mind's eye, I can still see him, leaning back in his chair, staring at me as if he is the devil himself.

"Well, congratulations," the redhead mutters.

"Thanks," I reply automatically as if I have actually won something.

I feel a touch on my shoulder and turn to see Catherine Moriarty. She is glowing with satisfaction. "Come with me."

I turn and follow her into a large room with stacked chairs and tables around the walls. She closes the door and turns to me.

"I knew I made the right decision with you," she gushes excitedly.

"What's going on? Why did he bid a *million?*"

"Judging from the amount of photographers out there, I'd hazard a guess it is a profile-raising stunt. I hear he has some bad publicity coming his way, and his publicist might have figured this would be a way of white washing the coming bad news."

"What does it mean for us... me?"

"Nothing," she replies calmly. "We change nothing. Follow the plan I've outlined. If you look into your banking app now you will see that the first payment should already be in your account. As agreed the next payment will appear when you successfully complete the exchange." She hands over the black purse slung over her shoulder. "The painting is in here, and the map of his apartment and detailed instructions will be in an email to you."

I take the purse and hold it awkwardly in my hands. "Will he call me about the dinner date?"

Her mouth twists. "His secretary will probably call to arrange a time and place."

I nod. "Right."

"Any more questions?"

I shake my head. To be honest, I feel quite strange and light-headed. As if all this is happening to someone else and I'm just watching.

"You have my number if you have any other questions or need clarifications on anything... and Raine... congratulations."

Then she leaves me standing in the middle of that deserted store room stacked with unused chairs and tables. I stand there for a while thinking of his eyes. They are cold and cynical. The eyes of a man who has seen it all and doesn't like what he has seen.

I have a feeling I am not going to like him, which is just as well because I'm about to steal his painting. There is a sick feeling in my stomach when the reality of the thought hits me. Until now there was a chance he would pick someone else, but this is it now. He picked me.

I'm about to become a thief.

RAINE

"Please be careful, Raine. If anything at all looks risky or not right just leave."

"Don't worry, Mom. I'll be very careful."

My mother wrings her hands anxiously. "Yes, yes, I know you are always very careful, that's your nature, but you will be extra careful tonight, won't you?"

"I'll be super careful, I promise."

She nods distractedly. "Do you think your neckline's a bit low?"

I laugh through the nervousness I feel. "If I dress like a nun, he's hardly going to invite me back to his place, is he?"

My mother takes a deep breath. "Yes, yes, of course. You look lovely, but maybe you should wear a necklace or a scarf."

I grasp my mother's hand in mine. "Stop it, Mom. The whole damn world knows I'm going out on a date with him, he's hardly going to try anything. Even if he catches me trying to steal his painting I don't think he will report me to the police. It'll spoil his big PR stunt."

My mother chews her bottom lip nervously. "You're right. Of course, you're right. But you will be careful anyway, won't you?"

"I will." I lean forward and kiss her cheek. "Now will you please stop making me nervous. It's hard to play the part of a Jezebel when your stomach is churning."

My mother cracks a smile, but her eyes fill with tears. She reaches out her hand and strokes my hair. "When your father left, I thought I would die. There were so many bills, so many debts. How was I going to bring up two girls on my own? But you know what. It has been a breeze because of you. You pulled your weight even when you were tiny." Her lips tremble, tears pour down her face, and her voice breaks. "You cleaned, you polished, you ironed, you made breakfast. And as soon as you were old enough you babysat, you walked dogs. You did anything you could to help me. And right now I feel like the biggest failure because you are going out to sacrifice yourself for this family."

"Oh, Mom. There is not a moment of the past that I would change. I did it because it gave me pleasure. I wanted to. I love you. Nothing is more important than you and Maddy."

"What's going on here?" Madison asks from the doorway.

"Nothing," Mom says, wiping her tears.

"Are you crying?" Madison asks.

"Of course not," Mom says.

"Dust in her eyes," I say.

"Whoa! Raine. You look beautiful. Is the dress new?"

"Yeah. A friend gave it to me."

"It's gorgeous." She comes forward and taking my hand swings me around. "You're going to burn the billionaire's eyes."

"Of course not. No doubt he goes out with far more beautiful women all the time."

Her thin, pale face breaks into a cheeky grin. "Then why did he bid a million dollars for you?"

"It is a publicity stunt."

"That's not what the papers say."

I shake my head. "How many times have I told you not to read those nasty gossip pages?"

She laughs, the carefree laugh of a teenager. "Anyway, I think he is delicious. Are you going to stay overnight?"

"Madison Fillander," Mom cries in a scandalized voice.

"What?" she asks innocently.

"Because I don't do one-night stands."

My sister's eyes narrow. "Why are you so sure it'll only be one night?"

"Because it's a purchased charity dinner date and anyway he looks like someone who is spoilt for choice. Someone who arrogantly takes what he wants and doesn't care about the consequences. He is not someone I want anything to do with."

She pulls a considering face. "If you really believe that, why are you dressed so sexily?"

"Do you think Raine should wear a scarf?" Mom asks immediately.

"No," both Madison and I reply in unison.

Then we both look at each other and laugh. At that moment, I know I am doing the right thing. I love my sister and there is nothing I would not do for her. If I have to steal a worthless painting from a billionaire so be it. If I have to go to prison and carry a prison record for the rest of my life so be it. Nothing is more important than keeping her alive. We are a unit. The three of us against the whole wide world. I feel tears burn at the backs of my eyes and blink them away.

There is no more nervousness.

This is just another job. I remember all those years ago when Mr. Jackson, whose daughter I was babysitting for, tried to kiss me. I just kneed him in the nuts. It hurt him so much that he couldn't even scream. His eyes bulged so much I thought they were going to fall out of his face. He just clutched his groin and sank to the floor with gasps. After that he kept well away from me.

I learned quickly that night what worked for Mr. Jackson would work for any man. If I had to knee Konstantin Tsarnov tonight that is what I will do.

"Right. I should go," I say.

"Good luck, honey," Mom whispers.

"I won't need it, Mom," I say softly.

She frowns. "I'll be waiting here for you."

"And me. Only because I want the juicy details," Madison says cheekily.

"You're not waiting up for anybody, young lady," Mom scolds sternly.

"For god's sake, Mom. I'm not a baby."

"On that note, I'm off," I say and start moving towards the door.

"Have a great time, Raine," my sister calls as I walk out of the door.

I turn back and see them both standing next to each other, my mother's face anxious, and my sister's face innocent and smiling, and again I know without any doubt that I'm doing the right thing for all of us.

RAINE

https://www.youtube.com/watch?v=6Whgn_iE5uc&
ab_channel=SantanaVEVO
Smooth

The cab Catherine had ordered for me, stops outside the swanky restaurant where Konstantin's secretary had arranged the date to take place. One doorman holds the cab door open while the other moves to open one of the double doors of the restaurant.

I thank them both and sweep confidently into the restaurant. The hostess comes to greet me. It is clear she immediately recognizes me from the many photos of me that have been splashed all over the press.

"Good evening, Miss Fillander."

"Good evening," I greet back.

"Mr. Tsarnov is having a drink at the bar. If you would like to follow me..." she trails off as her head dips almost in a bow.

I don't think anyone has been that reverent to me in my whole life. "Thank you," I murmur.

I follow her past a large dining room to a conservatory, where a private area has been cordoned off with gauzy curtains and plants. Konstantin Tsarnov is clearly no gentleman. He doesn't stand as we approach. Instead he lifts his glass to his arrogant lips, and takes a sip of the colorless liquid in it.

"Your guest, Mr. Tsarnov," she says deferentially.

He says nothing while a waiter seats me, then holds out a drinks menu for me. I don't take the menu.

"Martini, dry," I murmur.

"Very good," he says and flaps away.

I swivel my eyes back to the man opposite me. I have to suppress a shiver. His eyes are a cold, strange mixture of gold and bluish green. Like a wolf's. Wild and dangerous. He watches me expressionlessly. Being so close to him is like coming close to a power generator. I feel the hairs on my body stand with warning.

He puts his glass down on the table. "Hello, Raine."

The way he says my name has a bizarre effect on me. And shockingly not the effect I could have ever Imagined. It makes me want to grind my pussy against his mouth. Jesus, what the fuck is the matter with me? I avert my gaze away from him. "This restaurant is nice."

"Yes," he agrees.

I bring my gaze back to him. "So... here we are."

His mouth twists. "Here we are."

I bite my lower lip. Is he deliberately making this awkward? "Do you come here often?"

Now I clearly see the sarcastic amusement in his eyes. "No."

"Look, this is supposed to be a date. You're required to give more than one word answers."

"I'm Russian. We can't help it. We're stoic."

"Why don't you pretend I'm a billionaire and I have something you want to buy?"

The most interesting thing happens. His eyes flash and become almost liquid yellow. Wow! Fascinated, I stare at him intently.

"I've never met a billionaire who looks like you and has something I want to buy," he drawls.

I shrug, as if flirting with Russian billionaires is something I do all the time. "Then pretend I'm fat and middle-aged and grey-haired."

He laughs. A deep, sexy sound that touches me somewhere deep in my soul. How totally, utterly, complexly surprising. I try not to react.

"That Raine Fillander would be *very, very* difficult."

"Why?"

"Do you want the truth or the PC version of the truth?"

"Give me the PC version?"

"You have the face of an angel and the body of a stripper."

"That's the PC version? Do I dare ask for the truth?"

He doesn't smile. "You have a mouth made for blowjobs and a body ripe for fucking."

I feel the heat rush to my cheeks. Thank God, my martini arrives and I can busy myself with thanking the waiter and taking a sip. I swallow. "Did you have a good day?"

"Yes. You?"

I put my glass down. "My day was weird. Thanks to your little PR stunt I've become a sort of celebrity. People keep recognizing me on the street."

He looks surprised. "That's unappealing?"

"Should I find that appealing?"

He shrugs. "I got the impression everybody wants to be famous these days no matter what for."

I don't for sure, but I have other things I want clarified. "Other than the blowjob mouth and fuckable body, why did you pick me?"

His eyes never leave me and his voice is flat. "Because except for you every one of the other girls looked directly at me. I'm curious why they were all looking and you weren't."

An icy finger drags down my spine and I try not to shiver as I pretend to shrug carelessly and tell the first of what will probably be a whole bunch of lies. "One of the girls mentioned you. Said she fancied you, which made the other girls interested. They googled you." Then to stop any further discussion on this subject, I quickly raise my glass and say, "Here's hoping your million is put to good use."

He doesn't raise his glass. "It already has." His voice is quiet, his eyes expressionless as they watch me.

I take a sip and taste nothing. A waitress brings a small tray of four little appetizers. They look beautiful. I stare at them as she rattles off the spiel she has been told by the Chef. I pick the words glazed, tomato jelly, wild salmon, but everything else is a blur. She moves away. I feel as if I should go out, come back in, and start all over again. Somewhere along, I lost my way. He seems so unreachable, so foreign, so totally outside the kinds of men I usually deal with. How on earth can I make him invite me back to his house? I watch his hand, square and manly reach out. He picks up the ceramic spoon with the small bit of food loaded onto it. I follow his hand as it moves upwards. His mouth opens and the spoon slips into it.

He is hot. Really, really hot.

I swallow hard. I am completely out of my depth here. He is like nothing I have ever encountered before. Even though I dislike what he stands for, I can feel my body responding to him. Which is weird and uncomfortable. I don't want to want him.

But...

Madison needs the money. Somehow, somehow, I have to find a way to get to him, to get beneath this impenetrable wall around him. I know he thinks I'm sexy, I just have to play up on that. I lick my bottom lip and I watch his gaze follow the movement of my tongue.

Yes, that's more like it.

KONSTANTIN

Something's not right. She has a body made for sin and of course, the attraction is surprisingly potent, but there's something else going on in the background. She is *not* just a girl who took part in a dinner date auction for charity.

She's hiding something from me.

Emotions, many negative, flit through those beautiful, thickly lashed eyes. Then her teeth sink into that plump bottom lip and my attention is drawn to the holy sight like a moth to a flame. Intense arousal burns in my stomach as an image flashes into my mind. My cock buried in that swollen mouth. The image is vivid and raw and sexually jarring. Fuck!

My gaze drops down to her barely covered chest. Another image rushes into my head. Her legs wrapped around my waist, and my face buried between those full, heavy breasts.

My blood rushes away from my brain, and heads downward. My cock jumps into life, hard and greedy for a taste of Raine

Fillander. I wonder how she would react if she knew how hot and hard I am for her.

I stare straight into her eyes. Her breathing hitches, and she drops her gaze hurriedly.

"I have a question," I say softly.

She freezes, and it takes a few seconds before she is able to return her gaze to mine, a frigid smile across her face. She is nervous, very nervous about something.

"Yes?" she whispers.

"Did you know who I was before the auction?"

She shakes her head, and her voice is sure and somewhat relieved. "No."

"So why aren't you curious like all the other girls?"

Hot color runs up her creamy neck and turns her cheeks rosy. "I'd already done my own research," she answers softly.

"And you don't like what you found?" I ask, amused.

"Something like that," she admits.

"Which part doesn't suit you?"

She shifts uncomfortably. "I don't like what you stand for."

"Ah, a socialist. You don't like insatiable billionaires as a principle."

She draws her shoulders back, and I see angry fire come into her sapphire eyes. They become stormy with emotion. It's as if someone just tipped a wild leopard onto the chair in front of me. I stare at her with fascination. I'd love to see those eyes when she comes.

"I'm not a socialist," she says tightly, "but yes, I detest billionaires who lie, cheat and steal on their way to the top, then think they can make it alright by making a tax deductible million to a children's hospital."

Finally, she is not pretending, but if she hates cheating, lying, stealing billionaires who make donations for all the wrong reasons, why is she here dressed to kill? I take a sip of my vodka as I weigh my options. I'd very much like to fuck the living daylights out of her, but I'm also aware there is something else going on under the surface. I decide to call her bluff.

"You know, you don't have to stay. I'm quite happy to dine on my own."

With that the marvelous wildfire is instantly extinguished, and to my surprise, a mixture of fear and some other emotion takes its place.

RAINE

anic floods my body. Jesus, what the hell am I doing? This is not a date where I am free to sprout my nonsense about how unfair the world is! I'm here to save Madison. I drop my gaze quickly to the shiny surface of the table so I can regroup. I let my dislike of his status cloud my judgment, but I won't make the same mistake again. When I look up, my face is schooled into apologetic lines.

"I'm sorry. That is not fair. I don't know anything about you, or how you made your money. No matter what your reasons are for dropping a million on this dinner, it is for a good cause and the least I can do is fulfil my end of the bargain and be an interesting dinner companion." I lean back and give him my best smile. "Can we start again?"

His expression remains unreadable, his voice indifferent. "Sure."

The sheer relief almost makes me lean forward and thank him, but I stop myself in time. That would be suspicious. Fearful that there could be an awkward silence, I throw out the first question that comes into my head. "Do you ever go back to Russia?"

"Yes, I have many business interests there."

Not much to go on, but at least it isn't a one-word answer. "I've seen pictures of Russia, but I've never been."

"Of course you haven't. You're American."

I feel my back start to straighten and force my voice to be kinder. "What do you mean?"

"Aren't Americans taught to fear the big Russian bear behind the iron curtain?"

I shake my head. "Not at all. There are even a couple of Russian kids in my school."

Suddenly, he looks bored. "If you are finished with your aperitif, perhaps we can head over to our table."

"Yes, I'm finished," I mumble, hoping I haven't blown it. It's all gone so wrong.

He lifts a finger and a waiter rushes over. "My usual table?"

"Yes, Mr. Tsarnov," the man says obsequiously, as he bows and leads the way. Clearly, Mr. Tsarnov is a heavy tipper.

Konstantin stands as I do, and I see that he is very much taller than me. At least a foot and I'm wearing high heels. We walk towards the restaurant. I can smell his aftershave. Woody and expensive. And I can feel the raw power coming from his body.

We are seated at a table screened off from everyone else. I can see now what Catherine meant when she said he guarded his privacy jealously.

The next few minutes are filled with ordering our food. I am too nervous to eat, but I order a starter and a main course. Then the waiters leave and we are alone once more and my mind goes blank. All the subjects that Catherine had told me would be of interest to him are gone from my mind.

"Tell me about you," he invites suddenly.

The relief is palpable. "What would you like to know?"

He shrugs. "Anything you want to tell a date that is going nowhere."

I smile. "Well, since this relationship is going nowhere, I guess I don't have to pretend or impress and I can tell you the things I'd never dream of telling a real date."

"Yes, the lure of the one-night stand," he drawls.

"Do you think we'll end up in bed?"

His eyes glitter with interest. "Do you want to?"

"Maybe. Depends on how our... date goes."

An unfathomable expression crosses his face. "What needs to happen for you to end up in my bed?"

The words I never intended to utter tumble out of me. "Make me laugh. Make me understand I'm not going to feel like a slut in the morning."

He frowns. "Why would you feel like a slut in the morning?"

"I don't know. The only time I ever had a one-night stand I felt terrible. I left before he woke up because I couldn't bear it if he was indifferent."

He leans forward, his expression intense and curious, as if I am a species that is completely alien to him, and he's really trying hard to understand me. "Why would you care what he thinks?"

His question makes me forget to be a seductive nymph and I answer honestly. "I don't know and can't explain why, but it could be my conservative background. I can never just let my hair down, my brain is always thinking in the background. One of my friends once slept with a celebrity. She told me it was great, really fun. In the morning, they had breakfast in bed, she took selfies with him, and then she left. She has no regrets at all. In fact, she even considers it one of those events she will remember with pleasure and fondness when she is an old grandmother. Me, I can *never* do that. I don't like the idea of being a notch on someone's bedpost. I guess, you have hundreds of women lining up to have sex with you, huh? You have fun with them, then never give them a second thought."

"That's right. I tend to go for women like your friend. They are under no illusions. They take their pleasure and they leave." He leans back. "Whenever I make the mistake of picking women like you, it is always messy."

Shit! Why is it every avenue I go down takes me to a dead end? I look deep into his eyes, and whisper, "Perhaps tonight I want to be a woman who is under no illusions."

His eyes narrow with speculation. "Why?"

After a few false starts, I suddenly see the light at the end of the tunnel. If I play my cards right I can end up in his house as another one-night stand, then pretend to change my mind because of strongly held principles once I've switched the painting. It doesn't feel good, but it would hardly be the end of the world for him. A guy like him must have a black book full of names.

I shrug gently and smile seductively. "Because everything about you is wrong for me, and that surely must make you the perfect kind of guy to have a one-night stand with."

KONSTANTIN

Now I know for sure something is up. I play along partly because I'm curious as to where this is going, and partly because I can't help myself. The longer I spend with her, the more I want to fuck her. I watch as she cuts a tiny piece of salmon and slips it into her irresistible mouth.

"How did you come to be part of the auction?"

She looks down at her plate and swallows hard, as if it's not the smallest piece of salmon one could possible imagine putting into one's mouth, but a whole fucking frog.

Then she looks up and smiles. "I was bartending at a party and a woman from the agency that was supplying the dates asked if I wanted to be one of the dates."

"Hmm... you did it for charity, of course. No payment."

Her face becomes bright red, but she doesn't look away, and oddly manages to sound sincere. "Charity, obviously."

Then she changes the subject quickly, which makes me think *charity, obviously* is a half-truth.

"I saw when I researched you that you are very interested in horses," she murmurs, batting her eyelashes.

I try to keep my amusement from showing. Clearly, she doesn't flirt much. "Yes, I keep a stable in England."

"I used to ride a horse a long time ago. It's the best feeling in the world when you are galloping on a powerful horse."

"Yes, it is."

"Do you go to England often?"

"I'm going there tomorrow... want to come? We can go riding together."

Her eyes widen with shock, then she blinks, and stammers, "I... I... have to work tomorrow. Er... thank you for the offer... it... is very kind of you."

I smile pleasantly. "I wasn't being kind. I wanted to take you away for a... how do you Americans say? A dirty weekend."

"Oh!" She puts her knife and fork down. Somehow, I think she's finished eating. Not that she ate much.

"I... I have to work, otherwise I would come," she says with a frown.

"Relax," I drawl. "You're not the first woman who's turned me down."

She looks surprised. "Really? Do women ever turn you down?"

"Plenty, when I was younger... and a nerd."

"I can't believe it. *You* were a nerd?"

"Yup, I was glued to my computer screen day and night. Couldn't even look a girl in the eye."

She smiles, her beautiful sapphire eyes filling with relief that the conversation has moved away from her. "God, I can't imagine you being shy."

"I was not shy. I wasn't interested. I was so completely and utterly consumed with the thing I was creating I barely slept."

She leans forward, her face inquisitive, the creamy swell of her breasts tantalizing. "What were you creating that so consumed you?"

I stare at her warily. Her beauty is distracting and I'm itching to feel her skin, but is she from the enemy? I can't tell, but I won't take any chances. "Just a computer program. Would you like some dessert or coffee?"

She hesitates. "Do you want dessert?"

I shake my head. "I believe the chocolate tart is very good."

"Very tempting, but I'm not sure I can eat anymore."

I catch the eye of one of the passing waiters and make a writing motion with my hand, then turn back to her. "It's been a lovely evening. Thank you."

"I... uh... I wonder if perhaps I can have a drink at your place?"

I lift an eyebrow. "Drink?"

Hot color rushes into her face. Either she is an excellent actress or she has never done this before.

She takes a deep breath. "You know, one for the road."

"I have a party to go to tonight." There is a pause, then I hear myself say, "Would you like to come?"

She looks confused. "A party?"

"I have to say a quick hello to someone important to me."

For a second I think she is going to refuse, and perhaps it would have been best if she does. Then she smiles that sexy, sinful, smile and says, "Sure. Let's go to this party of yours."

And a very, very strange thing happens inside my body.

RAINE

A midnight blue Rolls Royce waits for us. The doormen rush to help us into the back. I have never been inside a Rolls before and I swear it is like sitting on a bed. It is so comfortable. The plush leather is smooth under my palm and the car is scented with some delicate perfume.

"Wow, this is nice," I murmur.

His phone must have vibrated in his pocket, because he takes it out and looks at it. "Please excuse me. I have to take this call."

"Go right ahead," I say quickly.

He launches into Russian. I turn to look out of the car. I can hardly believe the reflection in the window is me. I have never done anything like this before in my life. To be honest I haven't done much in life except work. There hasn't been much time for partying. I never let myself acknowledge it, but life has been hard. I listen to him talking and suddenly a weird thought comes into my head. How nice it would be if he was my man. If I could stop working so hard and just for a little while let someone else pay the never-ending bills.

Then I pull back from the thought.

He will never be mine. He and I are chalk and cheese. We wouldn't get on. Who am I kidding. He pretty much made it clear he wouldn't want me beyond a one-night stand or a dirty weekend in London. It's a silly thing, but when he invited me to go with him to London, I wanted to say yes. I wanted to say yes with all my heart.

But I can't. I can't.

I'm not here to have a fun time. I'm here to switch a painting. I'm here to save Madison's life. I hear him end his call and turn to face him in the dim light. He looks at me, then reaches out a hand to touch my hair.

"Is this color real?"

"Yes," I whisper, my voice hoarse.

He nods. "It's beautiful."

"It doesn't pay the bills," I blurt out bitterly. It's too late to take the words back, and in the dim light I see his eyes become wary again.

Shit. What the hell is the matter with me? Can't I just stick to the plan? I keep making the same mistake again and again.

"Are you a hooker, Raine?"

"No, I'm not," I deny hotly.

He leans away from me and the shadows make it impossible for me to make out the expression on his face. "What are you then?"

"I'm just a woman you'll never have to see again after tonight."

"Do you have many bills, Raine?" he asks softly.

For some bizarre reason, tears burn the backs of my eyes. I blink them away fiercely, and keep my voice dry and sophisticated, the way I imagine the kind of women he hangs around with would speak. "What doesn't kill you..."

"True," he murmurs from the shadows.

It's totally weird, but I can feel the heat from his body. And something else too. Sexual tension. It is almost like a daddy longlegs is walking on my skin, it's thread-like legs trembling. He is a total stranger, and one that I disapprove of, but I want to reach out and touch his skin, his hair, his lips... his cock. I shiver with the strong desire.

"Cold?"

"Not really," I whisper hoarsely.

He leans forward and touches a button, and the cool air coming from the air vent stops. He turns to look at me, and the discreet side light illuminates his face. Why, he is beautiful, really beautiful. Never could I imagine him as a nerd. Nerds are pasty faced and socially awkward. He is ruggedly gorgeous, chiseled face, masculine, sophisticated, and utterly confident of the place he occupies in the world.

"What is it?" he asks, one side of his lips curling with dry amusement.

I tear my gaze away from him. "Nothing," I say, turning my head. I take a deep breath and try to stop feeling gauche and school-girlish.

"Here we are," he says, as the car comes to a stop.

Before I can compose myself, the door is opened by an expressionless man in uniform. As I get out, he wishes me a cool good evening. Then Konstantin is standing next to me. Together we walk through the grand entrance of a block of apartments in what is one of the best addresses in Manhattan. The elevator is all shiny chrome and tinted mirrors, and smells of sweet vanilla. It transports us soundlessly up to the roof of the building.

The doors swish open and I have to still a gasp at the magnificent scene.

We are on the roof of the high-rise building. And it has been turned into a magnificent garden in the sky. All the miniature trees are hung with thousands of red paper lanterns, and against the night sky full of stars it is breathtakingly beautiful. The air is filled with conversation and laughter of the elegantly dressed guests. I immediately recognize a few celebrities.

A man in a black suit appears in front of us. "Mr. Tsarnov, this way please. The Count and Countess are waiting for you."

With one hand lightly resting on the small of my back, Konstantin moves us deeper into the party. I realize everyone is fabulously dressed, but in black and white. I am the only one wearing a blood red dress. People turn to stare at me: the men wear expressions that range from lust to amusement and the women unanimously show outright hostility, as if I have stolen their thunder by not following the dress code.

"It's a black and white party," I whisper to Konstantin.

"What does it matter? You look great," he says carelessly.

"Everyone is staring at me."

"Take it as a compliment," he says as we reach a couple.

For a second I am struck dumb by the flawless beauty of the man. He is tall and blond, which in itself is unusual, but what is truly amazing about him is his skin. It is so unblemished and pale he seems almost to glow in the light from the red lanterns. His translucent eyes alight on me and his red lips curve into a distant smile.

"Raine Fillander, meet Count Rocco Rosseti, and his wife, Countess Autumn Rosseti," Konstantin introduces.

"Oh, stop with the Count and Countess," the woman says to Konstantin. She turns to me and says warmly, "Please, just call me Autumn."

"Hello, Raine," the beautiful man murmurs, his voice low and hypnotic.

"Hello," I mumble, and not wanting to stare at him, quickly move my gaze back to the woman. She is pretty, but there is also something else about her that makes me instantly love her. She grins at me, then looks teasingly up at Konstantin.

"She's way too gorgeous for you," she says.

"I agree," he drawls.

I sneak a sideways look at him, and catch him looking at me as if he finds me irresistible. My toes curl inside my shoes.

Autumn laughs. "I predict your days as a bachelor are numbered, Mr. Tsarnov."

I feel myself flush with embarrassment. Thank god for the red lanterns.

"I'm sorry," Autumn says apologetically to me. "You must forgive me. I'm not being nosy and irritating, I'm just excited Konstantin has finally turned up with someone real for a change."

"Thanks for that endorsement," Konstantin says dryly.

"What? You're going to pretend you don't deliberately pick bimbos so you can pretend they are not right for you, and end it before it gets too serious," she challenges.

"I like bimbos." Konstantin's voice is light and easy. "Now can we talk about something else?"

She grins cheekily. "Of course we can, but I'm standing by my prediction. Your bachelor days are numbered, young man."

A man comes and says something quietly to the Count. He nods and says to his wife, "We must go."

She nods. "Rocco and I are flying back tonight, but you must come to dinner soon. Bring Raine."

Konstantin shoots a look at me and I raise an eyebrow at him. Without taking his eyes off me, he says, "Sure, I'll bring her."

"Good. Now we must be off." She smiles at me. "Have a lovely time tonight, Raine, and I look forward to having you to dinner."

"Thank you for the invitation."

"It would be a pleasure."

Autumn moves closer to Konstantin and kisses his cheek, but I see that she takes the opportunity to surreptitiously slip something very small, like a note or an USB stick into the palm of his hand.

Smoothly, he puts his hand into his pocket. "Have a safe flight."

For a second, I wonder what the thing she passed to him is, but then I catch myself. Clearly, they are all involved in something secret and I don't need to know. After tonight I will never see any of these people again. My life has nothing to do with this world of jet-setting exclusive people.

"Goodnight," the mysterious Count calls, as the couple turn away and melt into the crowd.

"Konstantin Tsarnov, is it not?" asks the wonderfully preserved woman standing to the right of us. Her eyes are hard and devoid of any warmth. In fact, there is something so frighteningly cold and calculated about her a shiver runs down my spine.

I feel Konstantin become tense next to me, even as he nods and says gallantly, "At your service, Mrs. Helena Barrington."

"I believe you know my son," she murmurs, a smile playing on her lips.

Konstantin's voice is smooth. "Yes, we're working on a charity project together."

Her mouth twists. "Ah yes, the Starlight project. Very noble."

"Perhaps you would like to be involved?"

Her eyes glitter strangely. "I'd love to, but I'm afraid I'm far too busy."

"Well, if you change your mind..."

"I believe you are leaving for London tomorrow."

Again, I feel Konstantin tense next to me. "Yes, how did you know?"

"I might have heard a rumor," she says airily. "When you meet my son, will you be good enough to send my love to him? Tell him to kiss my grandson for me."

"Yes, of course."

"Thank you," she says and turning, walks away, her head held high.

"What is that all about?" I whisper.

"I have no idea and I don't want to know. Come on, let's go get you a drink."

RAINE

uddenly, I don't want to be at this party. I don't want to spend more time with him or know more about him. I already know I will like him. I am already irresistibly attracted to him, and the deeper I fall for him the harder it will be for me to switch the painting. I don't want to feel guilty for the rest of my life. I just want to save my sister.

"Can we go back to your place?" I whisper.

He stares into my eyes, a strange expression on his face. Then he nods. "Of course."

"Konstantin, fancy meeting you here," a woman's voice cries gaily from behind us.

I turn to the sight of the sexiest woman I've ever seen in my life. She has jet black hair and is wearing a shimmering, skin tight dress that shows every perfect curve of her body. I instantly hate her.

"We are just leaving," Konstantin says coldly.

"What? You just arrived." She turns her stunning, sly eyes toward me. "This is Konstantin, all over. Such a bore. Always at his computer. Never wanting to party. Tell him you want to stay and party for a little while longer."

"Actually, I'm ready to leave," I reply.

All the fake friendliness in her eyes disappear and they glitter with resentment. I knew from the moment I set eyes on her that we would not get on and I'm right.

At that moment, a waiter arrives with a tray of flutes filled with golden bubbles.

"It's my birthday, Konstantin. Please have just one drink with me," she pleads looking flirtatiously up at him.

He frowns.

"Please. For old times sake?" she pleads.

"How is Bella?" he asks.

The question infuriates her so much her eyes flash and her jaw clenches, as she fights to control herself.

"Well, you always were more interested in her than me," she states bitterly. "Maybe that is what is wrong in our relationship."

Konstantin freezes, and his face fills with disgust. "You've become ridiculous, Chloe."

"Ridiculous? What is ridiculous is the way you are lusting after my six-year old daughter."

"I'm not *lusting* after your daughter," he grates tightly. "The only reason I ask about your daughter is because you fucking neglect her, and she is a lost little soul."

"Are you trying to imply I'm not a good mother to my daughter?" she huffs incredulously.

"Good mother? You wouldn't know how to be a good mother if your beautician slapped it onto your face and left it there for an hour. You're a lousy mother, Chloe. Absolutely the worst I've seen."

"How dare you? You arrogant, rude, conceited Russian dog," she snarls.

He shakes his head as if he is bored and turns to me. "Let's go."

"You think she's better than me?" she shrieks, throwing a furious look in my direction.

I'm aware that people around us are starting to stare at us.

"I know you get off on making scenes, but you're now wasting my time."

"Damn you, Konstantin. I give you everything. Everything," she cries dramatically.

"Whatever. Enjoy the party." He takes my hand in his, but as we start to walk away, a shrill female voice from the edges of the party screams, "Konstantin."

Both Konstantin and I turn towards the voice. To my shock, I see a young woman in a long white dress has climbed onto the wall at the edge of the rooftop, and is standing very still on it. The night sky is full of stars and she cuts a dramatic figure. The wind blows her flaming red hair across her face. When she lifts her hand to sweep it away from her eyes, her body sways dangerously. A collective gasp of shock rises from the crowd around us. Konstantin's grip around my arm tightens and I feel his whole body tensing next to me.

"Konstantin," she calls again, looking directly at him. Her face is very white and there is a strange, deadened quality to her voice. As if she is high on drugs or something. I've seen video montages of people on fentanyl who seem oblivious to danger or pain.

"For fuck's sake," I hear Konstantin mutter under his breath. "Wait here," he says to me.

I stand rooted to the spot as he starts to walk towards the woman. The crowd parts to let him through. As he gets a few feet away from her, she calmly lifts her hand in a halting gesture. "Don't come any closer," she warns in that dead voice. Then she reveals her other hand. There is a small knife in it.

Konstantin immediately stops and asks, "What are you doing, Alicia?"

"Why did you leave me?" she asks.

"Come down and we can talk about it," he suggests gently.

"No. Once I come down you'll just walk away. Just like you always do."

"No, I won't. We'll talk. I promise."

She shakes her head, making her red hair tumble around her shoulders. "No," she sobs pitifully. "I don't want to talk. I want you to want me again. Like how it was at the beginning. You said I'm beautiful. Am I not beautiful anymore?"

"Of course, you're beautiful."

"You're lying," she mewls.

"I'm not lying. You are beautiful, very beautiful." His voice rings out with sincerity.

Tears begin to pour down her face. "Then why don't you want me anymore, Konstantin?"

"Come down and we'll talk. We can go and get a drink together and talk."

"Can we go back to your place?"

"Sure."

She starts shaking her head. "You're lying. I can see you're lying. You came in with a woman. You're going back with her, aren't you? She's getting the Princess treatment tonight, isn't she?"

"Get off that ledge, Alicia. I'm not worth taking your life for. You're young and beautiful. You have your whole life in front of you."

"No," she screams suddenly, and slashes her forearm with the knife, the metal is like a hot knife through butter, her flesh rips open and blood squirts out of her arm like a fountain. Some of the women in the crowd scream at the gory sight. I stare in shock at what happens next.

RAINE

Quick as a flash, in the chaos that ensues, Konstantin lunges forward, grabs Alicia's hand and pulls her off the ledge. She wraps her arms tightly around him and begins to emit a strange high-pitched wail. Quickly, he unwraps her arms from around him and lays her limp body on the ground. He pulls his necktie from around his neck and ties it securely around the gaping wound.

"I love you, Konstantin," she mumbles, but it is clear that the shock and the loss of blood are starting to have an effect on her. She looks pale and lost. Konstantin turns and looks as if he is looking for someone in the crowd. When he locates the person or persons he nods.

Two men rush towards him.

"Take her to the hospital," he says.

The woman is so slight one of the men scoops her into his arms and carries her away.

Suddenly, the music starts up again, and a woman makes an announcement hoping the girl would be fine and urging everyone to continue partying. Konstantin walks up to me. He is covered in blood.

"Excuse me, while I go wash my hands," he says, with a frown.

"Of course, I'll wait here for you."

"Stupid bitch," Chloe says spitefully from behind me.

I turn slowly towards her.

Her eyes glitter with malice. "What?" she challenges. "You trying to take the moral high ground with me. You think you know him. You think you've got him. Ha, ha, let me tell you, that's what they all think at the beginning. Here's a piece of free advice for you, he will chew you up and discard you like a piece of gum so don't let him chew too long, or you'll become tasteless for all other men."

Then she turns around and flounces away.

I stare at the stars in the sky. All around me the party-goers are talking about what has just happened. I hear snippets.

"Did you know her?"

"Some model."

"Silly girl."

"Well, Konstantin Tsarnov *is* sex on a stick, after all."

I turn to look at the woman who makes the comment. It is impossible to tell her age. She is a walking advertisement for her plastic surgeon. She meets my eyes, hers are filled with wry amusement, and I turn away quickly. Even though the night air is balmy, a shiver runs through me.

Don't get involved. You have only one goal and that is to switch the painting and save Madison. Nothing else is more important.

"Raine," Konstantin calls.

I turn.

He has washed the blood off his hands and taken off his soiled jacket. There is a wet patch on his shirt. Otherwise you could never tell that moments ago he was covered in blood.

"Are you ready to go?"

I nod, and we walk towards the escalator. Neither of us speaks. Not even while we zoom downwards. I feel as if there is a stone in my throat. I steal a glance at him and find him watching me. His face is expressionless.

"No wonder you prefer your relationships to end before they start," I say. I had intended my voice to be light, but it comes out all high and squeaky. I try to laugh and that comes out all wrong too.

The doors swish open. I don't quite know how his driver is alerted, but the Rolls Royce glides to the front of the building just as we step out of the entrance. Konstantin opens the door for me and I quickly climb in.

I take some deep breaths as I wait for him to arrive on the other side. My heart is beating very fast. I feel like a thief. I clutch my bag tightly and tell myself everything will be fine. It's not like I'll be stealing his last meal or anything like that. He probably won't even notice the painting has been switched.

He slides in and closes the door.

"I'll drop you off at your place," he says.

"My place?" I croak. "I thought we were going to your place."

His eyes widen, then narrow with suspicion. "You want to have sex after what you've just heard and seen?"

I swallow hard. "Yes."

A strange expression crosses his eyes.

"What's your address?"

Automatically, I give it to him.

He moves forward, depresses a button, relays my address to the driver, then takes his long finger off the button again. Then he switches on the light and turns to me.

His eyes glitter like a dangerous wolf, but his voice is a lazy drawl. "I don't want to have sex, but there's no reason why you shouldn't have some fun."

He puts a hand on my knee. I can't move. I can't even breathe. Jesus, the man is about to have sex with me. This is not part of the plan. I should be jumping out of the car. I should be telling him to stop. I should be pushing his hand away. I shouldn't allow him to do this.

But I don't push his hand away,

I don't tell him to stop.

I don't jump out of the car.

I can't do those things because my nipples have hardened. Because I want to feel his hand move higher up my thigh to my hot, wet pussy.

KONSTANTIN

https://www.youtube.com/watch?v=tfSS1e3kYeo

Highest In The Room

She stiffens at the contact, but doesn't move away or resist. Neither of us has uttered a word. But her eyes speak louder than any words she could utter. She wants this! I look down at her plump lips and the image of Alicia's blood pumping out of her veins goes. All I see is Raine's generous mouth wrapped around my cock. My eyes glide across her face, her sparkling eyes, and her fair hair.

I know something is not right about her, about this situation we are in, but I'll figure it out later.

Without taking my eyes off her enormous sapphire eyes, I yank her knees apart roughly. She inhales sharply, but again she doesn't object. Little goosebumps appear on her skin as my fingers move higher and higher up her thigh. Then I slide my hands upwards while pulling her dress along until it ends up bunched around her waist.

She is wearing a sexy black thong.

I slip my fingers under the scrap of lace and she sinks her teeth into her bottom lip to stop herself from making any sound. Carelessly, I rip the delicate lace, pull it off her, and toss it away.

Her eyes fill with surprise and excitement, but she says nothing, does nothing. Just looks at me from those beautiful, beautiful blue jewels. I look down at her pussy. Spread open. Blonde curls. Pink. Swollen. Dripping. Delicious. Her smell fills my nostrils, and the desire to lick that sweet slit is shockingly strong, but I bring my eyes back to her face and lean closer to hers. I don't want to miss any change of expression from her.

My fingers dance along the soft skin of her inner thigh as I watch her pupils widen, and her mouth parts as her breath comes faster.

My hand brushes against the neat, soft triangle of fair hair. She squeezes her eyes when I touch her clitoris. It is engorged with blood. I'm not sure what's really going on in the background, but one thing is for sure, she is just as aroused as I fucking am.

I let my fingers wander lower to the slickness. My thumb remains on her clit, until without warning I plunge two fingers into her slit. She gasps, her eyes snapping open with shock. Her eyes stay glued to me as she tries to control her breathing. She doesn't expect my fingers to move so deeply inside her.

I'm not gentle. It's not what she wants. I'm the guy she detests. The guy that's perfect for a one-night stand. She's loving this rough.

I thrust my fingers in and out of her, hearing the loud sucking sounds of her wet juices on my fingers. Every few thrusts, she grunts or takes in a gasping breath.

With one hand I hold her steady while my other fucks her harder and faster. The walls of her pussy begin to tighten. She is so close now. I stare at her. I want to see the look on her face when I bring her to orgasm.

Finally, a low moan escapes her lips.

My thumb rubs against her hardened clit while two fingers search for her G spot. The way her eyes widen and become glassy tells me that I've found it.

She grabs my shoulder and squeezes. I know that she can't contain herself much longer. She clenches her jaw and looks away momentarily, only she can no longer control herself. Her eyes roll back. Her body becomes limp for a moment, but that doesn't make me stop, because I know that she's ready for something bigger.

Soon she will... come again.

And she doesn't disappoint. She lets out a loud scream and her body buckles and then shakes uncontrollably. Her thighs crush my hand, and her toes curl. She gushes onto my hand as the waves come and come, but I don't cease the hard thrusting of my fingers, not even for a moment. She groans and begs me to stop, moans that she can't take it anymore, but I don't stop.

I know she can take more.

Her body is still shaking as her pleading drops to soft whimpers. Her body becomes limp and her breathing is heavy and ragged, but now I notice that as much as she is trying to avoid staring at me, she can't. Our eyes lock. There is a strange expression in her eyes. I extract my fingers from her pink pussy.

I want to taste her orgasm from my fingers, but doing so would make me want to fuck her. I am fully erect, but I *choose,* I force myself not to do anything about that. Not now. Not yet. Not until I know what her game is. I remove a few tissues from the holder and calmly wipe between her legs.

This is called self-control.

She does not move. She just stares at me with half-closed eyes. Her legs are still spread wide open and I can see her pussy and how beautifully swollen it is. It takes all of my self-control to not fuck her right there. Instead I pull down her dress.

"We've arrived at your place," I murmur.

She turns her head in surprise, then turns bright red.

"I'll send someone to pick you up tomorrow at 8.00am."

"What?"

"You're spending the weekend in London with me."

"I... er... I can't. I have to work."

"Call in sick," I say carelessly. Something tells me she will be coming to London. I have something she wants and it's not my dick.

I rap on the partition, and my chauffeur immediately gets out and opens the door on her side. She looks confused and embarrassed.

"Goodnight, Konstantin," she mumbles, as she turns to get out of the car.

"You forgot your purse," I say holding out her bag.

She whirls around suddenly, her face anxious. "Oh! Er... thanks." Then she scrambles out.

"Goodnight, Raine," I call as the door closes.

As my chauffeur accompanies her to her door, I dip my finger into a drop of juice that glistens on the leather seat. I bring my finger to my mouth and lick it.

Raine Fillander tastes like heaven.

RAINE

My face is flaming with embarrassment as the expressionless chauffeur escorts me to the entrance of my apartment block. It is very possible that the back of such an expensive and luxurious car is soundproofed, but what if it isn't? What if he heard my moans and screams?

"Goodnight," I say, as I quickly open the door and slip into the building without actually meeting his eyes.

I hear his footsteps die away as I stand in the middle of the foyer. I know my mother will be waiting to speak to me and I don't want her to see me like this. My hands are clutching the bag with the painting so hard my knuckles show white. I unclench my hands, take a few deep breaths and try to calm myself.

He wants me to go to London with him.

I want to go. God, how I want to go with him. It would be a dream come true to travel to London. I've never done anything like that before. The years are passing me by and all

I ever do is work. I'd love to have a dirty weekend in a foreign land with a man like that. My passport has no stamps on it at all. It stares at me balefully.

What harm can it do to go with him? I've never called in sick before. It would be okay to do it just this once. And then I think of the money I need for Madison. And a thought occurs to me. Konstantin is so insanely wealthy. $120,000 will be nothing to him. Hell, he thought nothing of paying a million for a publicity stunt. What if I give the $50,000 back to Catherine's client, and ask Konstantin for a loan of $120,000? I can explain to him about my sister's medical situation.

He is a self-made billionaire so he almost certainly either stepped on or swindled a lot of people to acquire his billions, but I don't know why, maybe the way he seemed to care about Chloe's daughter being left alone too often makes me feel sure he will lend me the money if it is genuinely for a good cause. I don't want him to give me the money. It will just be a loan. I'll pay every cent of it back.

I hear the sound of the elevator arriving at the ground floor and I walk towards it. Two women get out and I walk in. I feel calm and sure of my course of action. I put the key in our door and walk into our tiny one-and-a-half room apartment. I call it that because Mom and Maddy share the normal sized bedroom and mine is barely bigger than a cupboard. My mother is sitting in front of the TV. As soon as she sees me she mutes it and stands, her hands tightly clasped in front of her.

"What happened?"

I shrug as casually as I can. "Nothing happened. We had dinner, afterwards he took me to a party, then he gave me a lift home."

My mother sags with relief. "Good. That's good. You didn't go through with it."

"No, Mom," I say quietly, "but I'm going to spend the weekend with him in London."

My mother's jaw drops in shock. "What?"

"He invited me to go with him and I said yes."

"But..."

"But nothing, Mom. It's just a weekend away. It's something everyone my age does all the time."

Mom presses her lips together. "You hardly know the man."

"Yes, it will be the perfect time to get to know him then, wouldn't it?"

A sound of defeat escapes her. "What about the $50,000?"

"I'll call Catherine on Monday and arrange to return it." I don't tell her about my plan to borrow the money from Konstantin. A) she won't like the idea. B) Konstantin might say no to me. I will only tell her if he agrees to give it to me.

"Yes, yes, you must return it."

I nod. "How's Maddy?"

"She's fine. She went to bed about an hour ago. Do you want a mug of hot chocolate?"

"Nah, I'm bushed. I'm off to bed. Someone is coming to pick me up at 8.00 am in the morning."

"Raine," my mother calls, a frown on her face. "Can you trust him?"

My answer is immediate and comes from somewhere deep inside me. "Yes. I can trust him."

My mother nods, but her forehead is still creased in a frown. "But are you sure it is a good idea to go away with him so soon?"

I smile at her. "It may be a terrible idea, but it's called living, Mom. Taking risks and going for it."

My mother looks at me sadly. "There was a time I thought like that. It is a beautiful feeling. The whole world was my oyster. Everything was possible. Everything was a wonderful adventure. It's sad when that feeling goes. I don't mean to smother you, honey. You go. Go and have a wonderful time."

I walk up to her and hug her. "I love you, Mom."

"I love you too, honey. I love you too," she whispers in my ear. "You go on to London and have the best time of your life. You deserve it. You're a good daughter, Raine. A very good daughter and I don't want you to ruin your life because you're trying to save Maddy."

"I'm not ruining my life, Mom. I *want* to go to London."

She searches my eyes. "With him?"

"With him."

She nods. "Okay, but I'll miss you like mad though."

"It's only the weekend, Mom."

"Yes, yes. I guess you're all grown up now."

I smile. "Don't tell me you just noticed."

She smiles back. "I've been pretending not to notice."

"Don't worry about me, Mom. I'll be fine."

"I know. Off you go to bed, then," she says with a resigned sigh.

RAINE

I can't sleep to start with. I keep thinking of the expression on his face as he fingered me in the car. Just thinking about what he had done to me and the way he did it, makes me so horny I have to masturbate.

But unlike the long-lasting explosion of a climax in the back of his car, this one is a quick, light burst that leaves me unsatisfied and craving more. I long to feel his cock moving inside me. The weird thing is I have never lusted after a man the way I am wanting him. Eventually, I go to sleep with these thoughts and dream that he has caught me switching the painting. His eyes are cold and furious. I'm so horrified I wake up in a cold sweat. For a long time, I lie in bed, staring at the ceiling, my heart beating fast.

It's okay, Raine, change of plan, remember, you're not switching the painting anymore. You're just going to ask for a soft loan.

When my heartbeat slows down, I try to go back to sleep, but can't even though it has been a long and stressful day and I should be exhausted. I'm too excited about my trip to

London. I toss and turn for ages until I give up trying to sleep, and reach for my phone instead. I begin finding out everything I can about the ancient city of London. I make notes about the places I want to visit, and it is the early hours of the morning when I finally fall asleep.

The alarm wakes me up, but I find myself instantly awake and buzzing with excitement. Quickly, I pack a small suitcase, filling it with my best clothes and my sexiest underwear, then I go to have breakfast. Mom is in her room getting ready to go to work, and Maddy is sitting at the kitchen table flicking through her cellphone. Her hair is still patchy on top of her head. She looks up when I enter our small kitchen.

"How was the date last night?" she asks, her eyes bright with curiosity.

"It was fine. How do you feel this morning?" I reply as I reach for a bowl in the cupboard.

"Fine? That's all I get."

"We had dinner, then he took me to a party and brought me straight back here."

"Hey, hey, back up, back up. He took you to *a party*?"

I take the seat opposite her and pour cereal into my bowl without looking at her. I feel sad for her. It's been years she has not been strong. The last party she went to is when she was fourteen or fifteen. Her teenage years where she should be out partying and having fun are passing away. All she ever does is stare into her phone for hours and hours. It is as if she has been sucked into a digital world. Even all her friends are digital avatars and they in turn know only her avatar. I pour milk over my cereal and look up at her.

"We didn't stay long. There was a woman there who tried to kill herself. It was quite dramatic. We left soon after."

She leans forward. "You went to a party where a woman tried to kill herself?" Wow! How?"

"She was going to jump off the edge of the roof of the building."

"What stopped her?"

"Konstantin pulled her off the ledge."

She raises her eyebrows and looks impressed. "Knight in shining armor in a billionaire's suit, huh?"

I shrug and put a mouthful of cereal in my mouth.

"She must be really brave. That's not how I would do it if I had to."

I stop chewing and swallow hard. The rough edges of the cornflakes scratch the insides of my throat. Then I look around in the direction of my mother's room, but her door is still shut. "Jesus, Maddy, don't say things like that," I whisper fiercely. "You're freaking me out."

"I don't want to freak you out, but it's true that life would be so much better for you and Mom if I were not here, wouldn't it?"

I grasp her thin wrist tightly. "Stop. Right. There. I won't hear another word of that nonsense. Now close your eyes." She doesn't obey and I raise my voice firmly. "Close your freaking eyes."

She closes her eyes.

"Now pretend I am no longer in the world, in this apartment." I give it a few seconds, then I ask, "What do you see?"

She opens her eyes and looks at me sadly. "It is horrible."

I stare at her intently, then tuck her pale hair behind her ear. "Exactly. We are blood, the three of us, we are a family, one inseparable unit, Maddy. If any one of us is gone, it would be an insufferable, intolerable, unspeakable loss. Do you understand?"

She nods.

"We will find a way to cure you. One way or another we'll get you back to health. So no more defeatist crazy talk, okay?"

She nods. "Okay."

I let go of her. I have grasped her so hard, my fingers have left white fingerprints. I have no appetite, but I put another spoon of cereal into my mouth and chew it, even though it feels like sawdust in my mouth.

"Raine?"

"Yeah?"

"Do you really think I'm going to get better?"

I smile at her. "Yes, I really, really do."

She smiles back at me. "Good. Because I'd love to go to a real party."

"You will. I promise."

"I believe you."

"By the way, I'm going away for the weekend," I say casually.

"Where to?"

"London."

"London!" she screams. "London, England?"

"Yes, London, England."

"How?"

"I'm going with Konstantin."

Her jaw drops. "What?"

I nod. "Don't tell Mom, but it's just a dirty weekend."

She gasps with shock. "I can't believe this. You? You're going for a dirty weekend?"

I pretend to be offended. "Why? You don't think any man would want to take me away for a dirty weekend?"

"Don't be such a dork. You know you're stunning. It's just you're always working. You never stop to have fun."

"Well, I'm doing that this weekend," I say firmly.

"How are you going to tell Mom?"

"She already knows."

Her eyes widen. "What did she say?"

"She said go and have a good time."

"Mom said that?" she asks incredulously.

I grin. "She sure did."

RAINE

I am driven directly to the airport. Once there, his secretary, Mrs. Berkman, a dark-haired, bespectacled woman in her thirties is waiting for me. She gives me an efficient smile and takes me into the lounge where I find Konstantin working on his laptop. His green-gold eyes sweep over me in a way that makes my stomach clench inside.

"Hello," I murmur, as his secretary wheels away my small suitcase.

He nods. "We are leaving in ten minutes. Want some coffee or juice?"

I shake my head.

"Have a seat. I just need to finish this."

"Sure," I say, dropping into the seat opposite him. While he types with lightning speed onto his keyboard, I watch him surreptitiously. His eyelashes are too long for a man. They sweep over his cheeks in a way that is adorable. And when he types his mouth moves slightly. I watch those sensuous lips and feel a flutter in my belly. Suddenly, he snaps his laptop shut and turns those gorgeous eyes up to me.

"Done. The rest of the weekend is for fun and games," he drawls with a wolfish smile.

I swallow hard and cannot find one suitable reply in my head to that announcement. "Good," I finally croak.

His secretary comes back to ask if we are ready to board. To my surprise flying private is a whole different ball game to flying commercial. There are virtually no checks save the quick scan of our passports. We are whisked aboard a medium-sized plane where everyone we meet addresses us by name and is smiling and super polite.

Inside it is luxurious, but subtle. No gold trim or any kind of ostentatiousness that I expected a nouveau riche Russian billionaire to have installed. Instead, it is simply a comfortable mode of fussless transport for a man who guards his privacy jealously.

I settle into my cream seat just as an air-hostess comes bearing a tray with tall flutes filled with champagne. Well, that's one thing I've never had. Champagne in the morning. I take a glass. Another hostess comes to place a small vase of flowers on the little table between us.

"To a great trip," Konstantin toasts tilting his glass up to me.

Sunlight slants in through the window and falls on his eyes, making the green appear like translucent glass and the flecks trapped inside them like bits of gold. I take a deep breath. Something about him affects me like no other man ever has.

"To a great trip," I echo softly, and take a sip of the chilled bubbles. They explode on my tongue and fizz down my throat. I have to be careful or I will get very drunk very quickly and make a fool of myself. I am in a strange environment with a man I am deeply attracted to, but cannot fathom. I put the glass back on the table.

"Have you been to London before?" he asks leaning back, looking as if he doesn't have a care in the world.

"No. I've never left the States."

He smiles. "Then you will love London."

"Yes, I know I will. I spent all night learning about it."

"Any place you want to visit?"

"I have a whole list, but I do realize one weekend won't be enough so I'm prepared to cut my whole list down to just the Dungeon at the Tower of London and a trip around London on one of those open-top red busses."

"Don't you want to shop?"

"Er... no."

He frowns, his eyes full of curiosity. "Why not?"

I shift uncomfortably. "I kinda already have everything I want."

He stares at me as if I have suddenly grown a horn or never met a woman who has told him she already has everything she wants.

"What do you mean?"

I decide to be brutally honest. Especially, since I intend to ask him for a loan. "To be perfectly honest, I am saving up for something important to me so I'll skip the shopping trip, thanks."

His eyes never leave me. "I'm going to pay for your shopping trip."

"Oh!" I exclaim in surprise. I never expected that of him, but I won't take up his offer since I would much rather have the loan instead. "Uh, that's very, very kind of you. Thank you, Konstantin, but there won't be enough time anyway."

His eyelids come down over his eyes as if he is deliberately veiling them so I can't tell what he is thinking. Then he raises them again. "I will arrange for you to shop with one of my assistants. She will take you to Knightsbridge and Bond Street for a few hours tomorrow afternoon."

"It's not necessary—" I begin to say, but he cuts me off.

A glimmer of mischief comes into his eyes. "You only say that because you've never been to London. It is absolutely necessary to shop when you are there."

It would break my heart to spend money on shopping when I can put it aside for Maddy instead, but I realize it would be churlish to keep arguing. I will make him understand later so I smile graciously and say, "All right. I will look forward to it. Thank you. It is very kind of you."

"It will be my pleasure," he murmurs.

I take a sip of champagne. "Will we go directly to your house?"

"We'll spend tonight at the Claridges, and leave for my house in the country in Berkshire tomorrow afternoon after you're done with your shopping and sightseeing."

"Is that where your horses are stabled?"

"Yes."

I look out of the window. The sky is blue and full of fluffy clouds. I feel as if I am in a dream. A couple of hours ago, I was sitting in our tiny apartment eating cereal with Maddy while my mother got ready to go to her dead-end job where she works her fingers to the bone for slave wages. And now here I am drinking champagne on a private plane on my way to London! I turn to look at Konstantin. He seems as relaxed as a cat in a spot of sunshine as he sits there watching me.

His life seems impossibly glamorous. He flies to London for the weekend, pays for women to shop in Knightsbridge and Bond Street, stays in expensive hotels even though he owns a mansion in Ascot, which is less than an hour away. I know because I researched him and his home online.

The air-hostess comes back, her pretty face lit up with a broad smile and carrying a tray artistically arranged with brightly colored morsels of food. The food looks fresh and appetizing, nothing like the overcooked, limp fare in a compartmentalized plastic tray I was given the other time I was on a plane. Square plates are placed in front of us. Together with real silver cutlery and crisp linen napkins.

Our glasses are refilled, then the girls withdraw.

"Go for it," Konstantin offers.

I choose a glistening cherry tomato tartlet and slip it into my mouth. The pastry is buttery and the filling is deliciously sweet-sour.

"Mmm... *nice*," I say, picking a tiny smoked salmon bagel next.

Of course, it too is divine. Very soon my glass is completely empty, the tray is nearly empty, and I'm feeling drowsy and a bit more than slightly tipsy. Not surprising since I hardly slept last night and drinking champagne in the morning is not something I am used to.

"Why don't you sleep for a bit," Konstantin suggests, as he stands and puts my seat into a reclining position. It actually becomes completely horizontal. He covers my body with a silky duvet.

"Thanks," I mumble, snuggling into the soft material.

"No problem," he drawls, closing the shutter of the windows next to me. Then he moves away from me.

Cocooned in that wonderful bed high in the sky I drift off.

RAINE

https://www.youtube.com/watch?v=weRHyjj34ZE
Whenever, Wherever

I sleep for five hours. I turn my head and see that Konstantin is also sleeping a bit further down the cabin. Very quietly, I get out of bed and tip toe towards him. In the gloom he appears softer, perhaps even vulnerable. All that distance he deliberately puts between him and the world is gone. I remember again the little thing the Countess had slipped into his hand. He hides secrets. Then there is the painting, what he supposedly stole from someone else. I suddenly wonder what the truth of that scenario really is.

That is the reason he does not allow the world to get close to him.

Seeing him like this makes the butterflies flutter in my belly.

I want him. I really want him. My fingers itch to reach out and touch him. But of course, I don't. Instead, I take two steps back.

Suddenly, he opens his eyes and looks directly at me. And just like that I am frozen. I cannot move a muscle. It is as if I am hypnotized. I stare at him, taking him in, unable to tear my eyes away from his.

The darkness around us feels like a blanket that I want to pull even tighter around me. And in the midst of it all is his gaze... shrouded in mystery and a haunting depth that makes my heart jitter to a stop in my chest.

"Do you think about it as much as I do?" he suddenly asks, his gaze searing and unblinking.

I know exactly what he is talking about, I can feel the arousal dampening my sex, but I feign ignorance, a nervous smile trembling on my lips.

"What do you mean?"

"You know what I mean." His voice is raw and throaty.

"Uh... I d-don't think I do."

"I can hear your heart beating," he says. "It's fucking racing. Every time I come into the room, it goes into overdrive, and your cheeks flush because your body is burning. You want to be touched. You want me to take you, but that sweet ache makes you very uncomfortable, doesn't it?"

My mouth falls open.

And for the next few seconds every time I try to speak, my voice sputters like a dying engine and then gives up.

"You know what I mean?" he replies.

"No, I don't," I insist stupidly, even though I can feel my own arousal dampening the crotch of my jeans.

"Come here," he commands.

Like someone put under a spell, I take the two steps over to him.

KONSTANTIN

https://www.youtube.com/watch?v=mOjTweUPt3Q.
Wicked Games

The moment she nears me, my hands shoot out to grip the back of her thighs and pull her towards me. She loses her balance and falls on top of me. She is already in a state of arousal and her musky-sweet scent fills my nostrils. I feel them flare as I breathe her in deeply. God, I want to bury my nose in her sex. She is so fucking distracting.

"I mean it's about time you joined the mile-high club," I growl.

I know she is not what she says she is. I know I'm most probably falling for the oldest trick in the book. Hell, she even looks like a honey pot. What I'm risking is still unknown but I know I'm risking too much, and I did try very hard to stop myself, to talk myself out of this inconvenient lust, but like a fucking itch it just wants to be scratched. I cannot help myself. Even trying to numb the craze for her body is no use. She is like a drug. In my blood. Calling. Calling. Relentless.

All fucking night long.

My hand reaches for the junction between her thighs, and through her jeans, I grab her mound roughly.

This is just sex. She is just an annoying, distracting, unnecessary itch, and I'm going to keep my cock in her pussy for as long as it takes to get rid of this crazy itch. Because after this weekend, I *never* want to see her again. She came into my life as part of an orchestrated distraction, but solving one problem often creates another. And I don't need complications in my life right now and she is one big complication.

Her sexy mouth opens in a gasp of excitement at the rough claim my hand makes, and my cock pushes hard and heavy against my pants. She is stunningly beautiful. I watch her avidly, as her plump lips make an O shape and I almost come right there. Fuck, it's like being a teenager all over again.

Her eyes flutter closed as my thumb finds and presses on her swollen clit through the material. I move my thumb in a circular motion, and a moan escapes her throat, as her hips begin to writhe to the hypnotic rhythm of my thumb. Watching her squirm her soft body against mine is too much for me to take.

My hands move to her ass and clutching her tightly to me, I lift myself out of my horizontal position and get to my feet. She gives a breathless gasp of surprise at the sudden movement. Turning her around I put her on her back on the reclining seat. Jerking her legs open I bury my nose in her sex. The heady potency of her scent makes my body shudder.

Fuck, this woman is driving me crazy.

My mouth opens and I cover her pussy through the material of her jeans. Her hands find their way to my hair, her fingers like claws, grasping, pulling, sending sharp shards of pain into my skull.

I relish the pain.

Hurriedly, I unfasten her buttons, tug the zip down, and yank her jeans down her hips and legs. She has on the smallest panties I have ever seen and I have seen many, a white lacy scrap of delicate material that covers her peachy pussy. Her smell makes my head swim with lust.

I don't waste any time.

I tear the lace off her hips and hungrily suck her wet, throbbing, delicious sex, all of it, into my mouth. Greedily, I lick her first bout of arousal clean, my tongue lapping into every swirl of pink flesh, then sinking my tongue deep into her.

"Oh god," she gasps aloud, and desperately holds onto my head. I can feel her body quivering.

The bridge of my nose strokes the engorged bud of her clit as my tongue digs repeatedly into her, and the combined motion I know is the perfect preamble to how the next hour is going to go for her.

She makes a small mewling sound of pure pleasure. "Don't stop... that feels so good."

Stop? She doesn't know I'm starving, and I just can't get enough as I devour her. I lift one of her legs up, hooking the crook over my shoulder and double down on ravishing her.

At first I use only my mouth, but then my finger joins in the fun, one and then a second, and suddenly I hear a sound that is not pleasure. I look up and her face is winced in pain.

Frowning I look down. My fingers are stained red. Blood! What the... I freeze. It cannot be. It is impossible. She is a honeypot. Don't they have sex with loads of men?

And yet... she is a virgin.

A swarm of emotions run through me at that moment, but none of which I know how to address. I feel shock, but then it quickly dissipates. And then I am struck by a dizzying burst of delight. No one has ever had her! I will be first to enter her body. The idea of being the first man to possess her is primitive and raw. It brings out the hunter in me.

I raise my head and meet her sapphire eyes staring down at me.

"Go on," she says softly. "Don't stop."

"Are you sure?"

Her answer is to thrust her sex into my face.

Nothing could be clearer than that, and I immediately comply with her demand. I do however, make a note to be gentler with her than the wild pace I'd planned.

A few moments later, and she is twisting and crying out with pleasure as three of my fingers work inside her while my mouth sucks on her clit. The gyration of her hips is mesmerizing and our rhythm is one of almost deranged frenzy and harmony.

"Oh God, oh God," she cries. Her husky voice is like music to my ears.

A guttural groan sounds from my throat. It surprises me. It is feral and has an animalistic quality. I recognize it as the sound of possession. The sound of a man claiming a woman. I feel her quickening, each hard precise thrust and vicious suck on her delicate bud bringing her closer and closer to the edge.

I feel as though I too am spiraling out of control as she races towards her own release. Her climax is almost upon her. Her whimpers are starting to sound like sobs.

"*Konstantin,*" she calls out. "Oh my God... oh my God."

She pounds her sex into my face, and when the last bout of pleasure sweeps through her body she breaks open. As her mouth opens wide, I slap my hand over it, muffling the scream. Her body shudders violently at the release as her juices pour over my chin in a stream of heated, molten ecstasy.

I lap up every bit of her release, every cell in my body electrified. She is gasping breathlessly as her eyes roll back into her head, and it is a long while later before her breathing seems like it has somewhat come back under control.

"Holy fuck," she mutters. "I want another one."

I grin at her. "You're going to have a lot more than one more."

"Oh yes," she breathes, her eyes shining.

She runs her hand through my hair and then cups my face. Lifting herself forward, she shoves her tongue into my mouth and drinks me in with an almost inhuman fervor.

I push her back on the seat and crush her body with mine as I cover her neck in sensual kisses. Then I bury my nose in the crook and inhale her scent.

She grinds her hips to mine, and when her hands move to the waistband of my pants to pull it down, I let her. Her hands tremble as she fumbles ineffectively at my belt, and it endears me even further to her. It's her first time of undressing a man, for fucks sake. I work it myself and my rock-hard cock pops out.

"Oh," she gasps, her slim hand reaching out to touch my dick.

My dick jumps towards her.

"Oh," she breathes again, her hand withdrawing automatically with astonishment.

To be honest even I'm surprised to find how hard and hot I am for her. Veins line the thick shaft, and the tip is already wet with the small white pearl of my seed. I rub the head, almost fascinated myself by its eager reaction to her. The creamy discharge is spread all along my shaft as I run my hand up and down the length.

A rush of pleasure begins to broil in the pit of my stomach at my own stroking, and when I lift my gaze to hers, I see that she too is transfixed.

"You are so huge," she whispers, as she reaches out her hand.

I take my hand off, steadying myself for when her delicate hand would come in contact with my hardness.

The moment her soft hand grabs a hold of me, I swear, I nearly come and have to clench my jaw and distract myself with an ugly thought to stop myself. She strokes my cock at first with unsure, shy strokes but very quickly, she finds a rhythm and boldness that turns her touch into pure torture. I rest my forehead against hers, unable to maintain any sort of pretense of detachment.

"You're so freaking big," she whispers again into my ear. "What if you tear me?"

I kiss the corner of her eyes. "I won't tear you. I'll take it easy, but one way or another I'm going to get all of me into you. This weekend this dick is going to be inside your pussy, your mouth and your ass. Many, many times."

Her eyes widen. "Yeah?"

"Yeah."

Her hands move from my cock and grab onto the taut flesh of my ass. "Go on, then. Fuck me," she dares, her eyes shining with challenge.

With a finger, I lift her chin so that my lips can meet hers, and molding my body to hers I kiss her, deeply and thoroughly, my tongue teasing and stroking hers in languid smooth strokes. Without breaking the kiss, I reach for the pocket of my pants, remove a condom from it, break it out of its packet, and slip it on me. Grabbing the head of my cock, I position it at her entrance and slowly thrust my hips forward.

"Let me know if it gets too painful," I whisper against her mouth.

She nods, recapturing my bottom lip. She sucks softly on the flesh, as her body tries its best to accommodate the hard flesh that is slipping into it. She is as tight as a clenched fist and I worry about tearing her.

I've never been with a virgin before so I go as carefully as I can possibly be so as not to hurt her.

"I'm fine, Konstantin," she rasps impatiently. "Keep going. Don't stop."

She thrusts her hips forward so that she can take a bit more of me, but at the slight gasp I freeze once again.

"I'm fine," she whispers and kisses me. "More. Give me more."

I move, my thick shaft inching its way into her, stretching and filling her walls. Eventually I ready myself for the final shove.

I cover her mouth with mine, then I push my hips forward and completely impale myself inside of her tight, wet heat.

RAINE

"Oh wow," I gasp, looking at him with wonder. Having him inside me is the most fabulous feeling in the world. I feel unbearably stretched and yet the sensation is one of satisfaction, completeness, and pure pleasure.

He begins to pull out of me again, and at the smooth slide out of me, pleasure coupled with the most agreeable twinge of pain arrowed straight to my core. I gasp aloud, my eyes widening at the indescribable sensation.

The urge to feel his skin on mine overwhelms me. Half crazed with lust, I grab onto the tails of his shirt and push the material almost desperately off his shoulders. Soon his bare tanned chest is on display before me.

He is just as I imagined him. Beautiful. Perfect. Manly. Silently, I curse the dimness of the space we are in. My fingers splay across his chest. I move my hand across his hairless, silky smooth flesh and smile when my palm graze his hardened nipples. I lean forward to catch the taut peak between my teeth.

He suppresses a shiver.

I begin to suck. Hard.

"Fuck," he breathes, and plunges into me swiftly in one smooth movement.

My back arches at the assault. My fingernails claw into his back and my whole body jerks as the acute blast of ecstasy that shoots through me registers.

"Are you okay?" he asks once again.

I bite down on his shoulder. "Don't stop. Move," I groan.

He doesn't need telling again, he rams into me over, and over again. His balls slap against the curve of my buttocks, while his hand reaches down to torment my already swollen clit.

I pump my hips to meet his ruthless thrusts into me, and with every thrust I feel myself branded, the taut walls of my sex sheathed like a second skin around this godlike cock. There is a spot inside of me that he hits over and over again, and the sweet tension it wreaks through my body leaves me feeling as though I have been run over.

I tighten more and more around him, frantic and panting, my cries echoing through the abandoned cell. I have long lost awareness of where we are and uncaring of anything beyond the magic of his possession.

His groans in my mouth, gruff and deep revs me on like an engine. Once again, the quickening of my entire core grows in intensity as we chase our impending and much longed for release.

My arms tighten desperately around him as my hips rock madly to the deep, rippling drive of his cock. In no time I feel my walls begin to convulse around him.

Tears fill my eyes as an unbelievable wave upon wave of a deliciously decadent climax washes over me. The experience leaves me nearly unconscious and I cry out in complete abandon, calling out his name.

He comes then, with a growl, a sound deep in his throat and so utterly possessive and masculine, something inside me instinctively responds by pressing myself against him and burying my face in his chest. It is a submissive gesture, a woman responding to her man at the most base level.

"Fuck," he mutters over and over, but I'm long past words. It feels as though my entire body has shut down, but at the same time it is brimming with a violent rush of pleasure that is strong enough to knock me out.

In fact, for some moments, it feels as if my brain is scrambled into mush, and I completely lose my awareness of where we are high in the sky and in heaven.

But then it registers that he is withdrawing from my body. I know I should pull my legs shut and get my jeans back on, but I am unable to move. My limbs are like jelly. I look up at him from under my lashes as he takes the condom off and pulls his pants on, before turning to look at me.

A strange expression crosses his face as he looks down on me. Then he shakes his head and wonders aloud, almost to himself. "How is it possible that I want to fuck you again so soon?" He bends down and slipping his hands around my ass as if I am a bowl, he slips his tongue into me.

I moan softly, and he begins to suck, lick, and nibble on me all over again. He doesn't stop until I climax again. This time the climax is so hard that my body jerks convulsively against his face and my juices shoot into his hungry mouth.

RAINE

We don't speak much. He seems to be preoccupied with something. After a while he even takes a sheaf of papers from his briefcase and begins studying them. It's a good thing because I'm not up to making any kind of conversation. I think I'm too shocked and astonished by how my body reacted to him.

The private air hostesses obviously understood when to interrupt and only come into the cabin thirty minutes later to bring hot towels.

They don't meet my eyes, and I know they know what we've been up to. They have to be deaf not to. I should be embarrassed, but I'm not. I actually don't care. I feel utterly shameless. My clit is still so swollen it bulges out from my pussy lips. And when it rubs against the rough material of my jeans I have to stop myself from moaning.

God, I just want his mouth on me... and his silky-smooth, enormous, hard cock inside me again. The way he made me feel is addictive. He is addictive. Suddenly, I remember Chloe and the girl who had tried to jump off the roof and the thought makes me frown. I better get a hold of myself, or I'll end up a humiliating basket case like them.

Tea, finger sandwiches, and cakes are served.

Needless to say, *everything* is delicious. Half an hour after everything is cleared away, we start our descent. I stand at the top of the stairs and breathe in the English air. It must have just rained because it smells fresh and cleaner than New York.

We are whisked through a quick passport check before we are met by his chauffeur. Seems strange to me that anyone would have a chauffeur in every country where they own a home, but I guess that must be normal for billionaires. Apparently, our bags are already in the trunk of the dark blue Bentley, so we get into the back of the car and off we go.

Oh, I just discovered people drive on the wrong side of the road here.

I stare out of the window in awe. No Skyscrapers. There are rolling green fields around us dotted with grazing sheep! It all feels so unreal. To think that only a few hours ago I was in New York. Now it is thousands of miles away. Another world.

"How long before we get to London?" I ask.

He looks at his watch. "We'll be there by 7:50 p.m."

Eventually, the roadway gives way to a dual highway, which then becomes a big busy road.

"We are now coming into London," Konstantin murmurs.

He names the areas as we pass through them. Earls Court, West Kensington, Knightsbridge. London is as different from

New York as cake is different from steak. There are no skyscrapers made of glossy glass and steel anywhere. All I see are wonderful and often intricate stone masonry everywhere. The buildings are works of art, evidence of a form of expert craftsmanship that is lost forever.

"Oh my God, Harrods," I cry, as I recognize the iconic building lit up. I suddenly realize I'm behaving like an overly excited child and sneak a look at him. I find him watching me curiously.

"Sorry, I'm not usually so unsophisticated," I mumble, embarrassed.

"Don't be sorry. It is refreshing to see someone so appreciative of life. I'm afraid all the people I deal with take great pains to appear world-weary." His mouth twists. "It's not as charming as they think it is."

I smile shyly at him. "That's good. Because you may see many occasions when I actually spontaneously explode with excitement."

He grins back. It's the first time I have ever seen him smile so openly. Usually, he is distant, measured, wary. Almost as if he distrusts me.

I turn back towards the window. For some weird reason my heart is singing. We pass by Hyde Park, London's own Central park, and turn onto Mayfair and the car comes to a stop outside Claridges Hotel. There are art deco lamps on either side of the revolving doors. Two doormen in top hats, green ties, and long coats standing on either side of them come to help open our doors.

"Good evening, Mr. Tsarnov, Miss," they greet, their voices crisp, their accents deliciously foreign.

We enter a lofty cream and off-white foyer with the iconic Masonic black and white square tile floor. I look around me in awe. It is pure British pomp with a twist of art deco. Reminders of a more dignified age. The strains of violins playing classical music fills the air.

Apparently, there is no need for us to book in. Everything has already been arranged by his assistants, or Konstantin has some sort of standing agreement. He walks through the vast space like he owns it.

Between the tall pillars are tables with people sitting and eating and drinking. The sounds of the voices float over to me. I cannot see them, but it almost seems to me as if they would be dressed in clothes that belong to a different era.

And then we reach the elevator and it is really like being frozen in time. It is made of wrought-iron with a comfy looking seat and a uniformed attendant. He too greets Konstantin by name.

We are booked in a penthouse suite. It has antique furniture and a grand piano! To my surprise I find out the suite comes with a personal butler. My gaze takes in the vases of fresh flowers and the bucket of champagne on ice laid out on one of the tables. While Konstantin deals with the butler, I walk over to the terrace. It has a superb view of London. It is nearly eight o'clock, dusk is falling over the city and the air is getting chilly. I can hardly believe I am here. It feels like a dream.

I take my phone out and text my mom.

Arrived in London.
In the hotel now.
It's fantastic, mom. Just fantastic.
I know u are at work now.
Skype me when you get home?
I love, love, love you. xxxx

RAINE

I hear a sound behind me and turn slightly. Konstantin is walking towards me. In his hands he carries two champagne filled flutes. He holds a glass out to me. This truly is the champagne lifestyle.

"May your trip to London be memorable."

"It already is," I murmur. "To be honest, it is the most exciting thing that has ever happened to me."

He frowns. "Really?"

I nod and take a sip.

"How old are you?"

"Twenty-three."

His eyes never leave mine. "You never found anyone to lose your virginity to?"

I'm not about to tell him, I've never had the time. Ever since I was fifteen Madison has been in and out of hospital and Mom and me have been working all the hours God sends to pay her medical bills. I even left school early to bring in more money into the household.

"Nope," I say with a grin that I hope will put matters to a rest.

"Hmmm," he says thoughtfully. "We should get ready for dinner. Our table is booked for eight thirty."

"Where are we going? What should I wear?"

"It's just a private club around the corner from here. So nothing too fancy."

My eyebrows rise. "Just a private club for billionaires?"

To my surprise a slight tinge of color touches his cheekbones. I have embarrassed him.

"Something like that," he mutters, and quickly changes the subject. "There are two bathrooms. You can get ready in one and I'll use the other." Then he moves away.

I turn back to the magnificent view of London and take another sip of champagne. Sounds of people from the street below filter up. As the bubbles burst on my tongue I try to memorize the moment in my head. For the rest of my life I will remember this amazing moment when I stood on the rooftop terrace of the world famous Claridges hotel and drank champagne on my own.

Ten minutes later, I've showered in the fabulously luxurious marble bathroom, and smelling of the mango and passion fruit shower gel, I slip into my black dress. It is a second hand buy, but it is of good quality with a classy slim silhouette. I zip up, brush my hair, and put on my make-up. Mascara, red lipstick, and the look is complete. Stepping into thin gold sandals, I go to the living room.

Konstantin is standing on the terrace balcony looking out over the city. He is dressed in a charcoal suit.

"Hey," I whisper.

He turns. For an instant I see a flash of something in his eyes, then the look is gone, replaced by the cool, distant expression he usually sports.

"You look beautiful," he compliments, his voice smooth, deep, powerfully masculine. No wonder all those women go crazy for him.

"I hate it when you steal all my lines," I whisper.

He walks up to me. "Think I'm beautiful, huh?"

"Yeah." I reach out and palm his crotch. He is as hard as a rock. "Wow! You're happy to see me."

His nostrils flare. "All the time. All the fucking time."

"Do you want to miss dinner and let me take care of this little problem?"

He shakes his head. "Don't worry, it'll keep until after dinner. I've got a long night of fucking planned for you, little Raine. You'll need to be fed and full of energy for it."

"Mmm... I can hardly wait."

The club is so close by we walk to it. It has no bouncers standing outside it, or velvet ropes. It is a discreet door, which opens as if by magic as soon as we approach it. Inside a man greets Konstantin by name and takes us deeper into the interior. The sultry eggplant and red cocktail bar he seats us in has a cozy, intimate allure. There are candles in red glass jars on the tables. Some exotic music, perhaps Japanese or Oriental, is playing softly in the background.

A waiter brings a silver dish with a butternut squash on it. Tucked into the hollow of the cooked squash, he tells us, is imperial Oscietra caviar. However, the squash is not just for ornamental purposes. There are little spoons with which we are supposed to peel the sweet buttery flesh of the squash and eat with the glossy black pearls.

A bottle of champagne is opened and our glasses filled with the straw liquid. I am struck by the waste. We drank one glass from a whole bottle on the plane, one glass each from the bottle in the room, and now another bottle has been opened. We are given menus to study. A quick glance tells me that the food here is going to be nothing like anything I am used to.

Game terrine with crab apple jelly, Cornish crab salad with rock samphire, Venison Wellington.

I also notice the menus have no prices. I suppose I should have expected that, with it being a private club and everything. I stare at him, mesmerized by the fantasy of being able to afford absolutely anything you want in life.

I lean forward. "Not knowing the prices of what I'm ordering is killing me."

He lifts a finger to summon a waiter. The speed with which the man arrives at his side is impressive. "Can I have a menu with prices for the lady, please?"

The waiter's eyes almost drop out of his head. "Of course," he mumbles, and scampers away. When he returns with a menu for me, his eyes are carefully blank.

I open the menu and learn that the price is fixed. It is £490.00 per head, which whoa, translates to $671.00. That's our family food bill for two freaking weeks. I look up at Konstantin and find him watching me, a speculative expression in his eyes, and I realize paying this kind of money for a meal is nothing to him.

At that moment, I decide to stop obsessing about how much everything costs, and simply be grateful for this unexpectedly marvelous gift from the universe. Anyway, it's only for a weekend and then it will all be over, but there will be no regrets, no hankering for more. I will happily go back to my usual life where every cent is carefully counted and hoarded away so Madison can have her operation.

Konstantin leans back in his armchair. "You said you were saving up for something important. If you don't mind sharing, what is it?"

I take a deep breath. It is now or never. This is the opportunity I've been waiting for. "I'm saving up for my sister, Madison's operation."

He stares at me stoically. "What's wrong with her?"

"She suffered several bouts of cancer, and now she needs to have a bone marrow transplant. The good news is I am a match and can make the donation which means the cost will be almost half. Mom and I have already saved $92,000 and we are working towards another $118,000 more."

His eyes narrow. "Doesn't a procedure like that cost a lot more than $200,000?"

"Yes, if it's done in the States. I've found a reputable hospital in Brazil that will do it for that price. The real escalation in cost comes from the long stay, like two to three months, in hospital for her. That's what makes it impossible for us to get it done in America. The plan is for the three of us to fly out to Brazil. I'll make the donation. There will be side effects, nothing long lasting, but things like nausea, back and hip pain, headaches, dizziness, fatigue, muscle pain. It means I'll need a few days to recover. Once I'm back to normal I'll leave Mom to stay on and take care of Madison while I fly back and keep earning money to make sure all the bills are paid and—"

I stop abruptly because he is beaming at me. His face is filled with pure joy. It is as if I have told a homeless man that he has won the lottery and is now a multimillionaire.

KONSTANTIN

I know I'm grinning like a fool, and this is not at all the reaction anyone would expect when they are telling you about their seriously ill sister, but I can't help it. Something inside my chest is soaring. She's *not* a honey pot! This is the reason why I kept getting weird vibes off her. That's why she was still a virgin at her age. And that's why alarm bells were going off in my head the whole time. But all she wants is to ask me for my help. Obviously, I'll check out if her sick sister's story is legit, but my intuition is good and I'm pretty sure just by looking at how cut up she is that her story is heartfelt.

I wipe the grin from my face. "I'll pay for your sister's procedure."

Her eyes widen with shock. "What?"

"I'll pay for it. Isn't that what you wanted to ask from me?"

She recoils as if in horror. "No. Of course not. I honestly thought about asking you for a loan, which I will pay back in full as soon as possible, but I was never just going to ask you to pay for my sister's medical bills."

I shrug. "I am happy to pay for it on one condition."

"What?" she whispers.

"The procedure must be performed by the best doctors in the best hospital in America."

Her jaw drops. She snaps it shut, then opens it to say something, but nothing comes out, so she shuts it again. Suddenly, her eyes fill with tears, and she slaps her mouth with her hand. Tears start pouring down her face.

She jumps to her feet and looks around her wildly. "I'm sorry," she mutters. "Please excuse me." Then she turns and runs the way we came. I see her talk to a waiter who points her in the direction of the toilets.

She seemed so broken I wanted to crush her to me, but I didn't. I didn't because I don't understand what I'm feeling. I do know though that women don't affect me like this. Never.

A few minutes later she comes back to the table. Her eyes are red and slightly puffy, but she has herself under control again.

She sits down and looks me in the eye. "I'm so sorry, I didn't mean to embarrass you or anything like that. It's just been such a big burden to carry. I could never really talk to anyone about it. I didn't want anyone to think that I resented the sacrifice, because I truly didn't. If anything I wished I could do more, but you cannot understand how big the fear has been to think she could die because I couldn't earn enough money... and... and... no one has ever been so kind to us as you have just been. I couldn't possibly take so much money from you. You must let me pay it back."

I shrug. "I don't want the money back. I own watches that cost many times more than what your sister needs."

She blinks, then whispers, "Thank you. Thank you so much. I don't know what I can ever do to repay you."

It's all happening too fast and I am already far more affected by her than I care to admit. So I try to look wolfish as I utter the next words and keep everything on a sexual level. "Oh, I can think of a few things you can do."

She smiles suddenly and it is like the sun coming out from dark clouds. "Thank you again. From the bottom of my heart. You don't know what you have done for me and my mom."

Before I can answer her, I see Blake and his wife enter the bar. As soon as they catch my eye they wave and approach our table.

I stand to greet them.

RAINE

I turn back to see a well-dressed couple heading towards our table. The woman has long black hair and easily the most uniquely colored eyes I have ever seen. Perhaps it is the lighting in the bar, but they appear to be orangey gold. As for the man he has a cold, forbidding look.

"Hello, how nice to see you here," Konstantin greets politely. They turn towards me, "Raine, meet Blake and Lana Barrington. Blake and Lana, this is Raine Fillander."

"Hello, Raine," both Blake and Lana say. Blake's face remains aloof and detached, but his wife shoots me a genuinely friendly smile.

"Hello," I greet back shyly.

"I love your dress," she says softly.

She manages to sound sincere, but I blush. I can tell just by looking at her dress that it is wildly expensive and mine is a second-hand garment I bought a year ago from Facebook.

"How long are you staying?" Blake asks.

"Just the weekend. It's Raine's first time so we're doing the touristy thing."

"Right," he says.

"I have a message from your mother."

Instantly, the mood in the group changes. Both Barringtons become still.

"She wanted me to tell you to kiss her grandson for her."

Blake frowns and Lana pales, as if she is scared by the innocuous message. Blake curves his hand protectively around her.

"I have no idea how she knew I was coming to London," Konstantin continues, "but it would seem that she approached me at the Iserby's party simply to pass this message on."

Blake nods, his eyes veiled again. "Thank you for the message. I hope you enjoy your stay. See you in New York next month."

Then Lana steps forward and kisses Konstantin on the cheek, but I notice that she does exactly the same thing the Countess at the party did. She surreptitiously slips something into his hand before she steps back.

She turns to me, a polite smile on her face, but it is clear that she is now troubled and unhappy. "Have a wonderful time, won't you?"

"Goodnight," Blake says to both of us, and they walk away.

"It's getting late. Shall we go into the dining room and have dinner?" Konstantin asks me.

"Yes, let's," I reply, turning away from the departing couple and looking up at him.

His expression reveals nothing, but I know then, that the meeting with the Barringtons was not accidental. It was planned. That is what we are doing in this bar. Waiting for them to appear so Lana could pass whatever it was she slipped into Konstantin's palm.

We move to the dining room. It has dark wood panels and paintings of fox hunting on the walls. The lights are dim and the tablecloths seem to be super white. I eat my dinner in a daze. I think I still cannot believe I am not dreaming. I listen to his hypnotic voice and watch his mouth move and I think of it between my legs.

Before I know it, the meal is over, we are standing up, and walking out into the night air. The air is wonderfully cool. We stroll back to the hotel together, our bodies slightly touching. At the hotel, we go up the elevator, our bodies still touching. I can feel the heat from his. My stomach feels tight with knots.

We get to our suite and he holds the door open for me. I walk in, and suddenly, I feel his hand on my arm. He whirls me around, yanks me so I slam into his body, and catches my lower lip between his.

Whoa! What magic is this?

I can hardly believe what is happening. This is not just a kiss. It is nothing like the one he gave me on the plane—oh, no. This is entirely different. His mouth on mine, moving slowly. Drawing it out. Making me moan from a place deep down in my center, a place only he's ever touched. All through one simple kiss.

But it stays gentle only until I melt against him.

When he knows how lost I am, his hands slide around my waist. He presses them into my back and pulls my body closer to his. I feel his hardness acutely through my dress. I wind my arms around his neck to hold on as he slowly drives me crazy and my knees go too weak to keep me standing. His tongue slides along the opening of my mouth before probing inside, exploring me as fireworks go off in my head. He groans, his hands pressing harder, the need between us growing like a fire which threatens to consume us both.

I want it to.

Yes, I want it with every fiber of my being. I want his hands on me and his lips, oh, his lips, his tongue and all of it. All of him. All night long and into the morning, again and again. Like how it was high in the sky. I want to touch him everywhere and taste his skin and listen as he whispers my name in the darkness. My entire body seems to sizzle, and my nerve endings feel like they are tingling.

Every cell in my body is desperate for him. I don't know how I got here, but I feel like an addict. An addict for him.

KONSTANTIN

She brushes her fingers along my jaw and rests them on my lips.

I love the sensation of her soft skin. I curl my tongue around her fingers and suck them into my mouth. Her skin smells like mango or some exotic fruit.

She watches me, mesmerized. Then she leans into me and lets her forehead touch mine. Her fingers slip out of my mouth. Her lips touch mine as I pull her even tighter to me and wrap my strength around her. My kiss is bruising and my tongue unapologetic, as it thrusts into her mouth.

She sucks my tongue wildly.

She tastes of the white chocolate and strawberry mousse she had for dessert and something that is uniquely her. The taste of her makes me feel drunk with ownership. Enveloped in my heat, she surrenders her mouth beautifully, welcoming my savagery. She's mine and I want all of her. I savor the sense of power I get from her total submission.

I'm totally and utterly crazy for her body. I know that now.

I hold her in place while my palms skim her curves. She moans into my mouth and I squeeze her hips. She slides her palms over my shirt and I deepen the kiss even more. My lips roam along her smooth jaw before dipping down to her throat. I suck the base of her neck. She whimpers and a bolt of pure, unadulterated lust shoots to my cock. I wanted to take it easy with her, but fuck... she is unbelievable. The effect she has on me is just unbelievable.

I pull away from her and look down at her. She's panting and her eyes are burning with need. With a groan, I touch her face. Her skin feels hot and satiny.

"Do you have any idea what you are doing to me?"

"No, but I hope it's like what you're doing to me," she whispers hoarsely.

I pull down the zipper of her dress and push it down her body. It is one of those dresses with an inbuilt bra. Her gorgeous big breasts spill out. Oh, fuck! For a few moments, I stare greedily at those ripe breasts, at the sexy satin body in those small panties, then I dip my head and grab one ripe breast, taking its rosy nipple between my lips. I suck it hard and her flaring hips move restlessly.

"Oh, Konstantin," she groans.

Her head drops back exposing her creamy throat. I growl at the delectable sight. With the last grip on my sanity gone, I lose track of everything but the swollen nipple in my mouth. Clinging to me, she moans sweetly as I carry on sucking. With my eyes, my fingers, my tongue and my body I plan to tell her that she is mine.

I will explore her body until there is not an inch left unclaimed.

I suck on another area of her neck and she lets me. We both know there will be blue marks on her skin tomorrow... to tell everyone that she is mine.

She pulls away suddenly and gets on her knees. Using both her hands, she clasps the base of my cock firmly. I feel her hot breath before the silky wetness of her mouth envelops me. I revel in the warmth and sweetness of her mouth, as she eases the head of my cock between her plump lips, and slides her tongue along my burning skin making me growl. When she sucks my dick all the way in it bumps the back of her throat, she eases up a little to keep from gagging. But goddamn, what a little heroine, she dives right back down.

"Yes. Right there, baby," I encourage.

She sinks down further than before, until I feel my cock head enter her throat. Her body jerks, and she pulls up again. I feel her relax her muscles before she glides her mouth down again. She gets a little further down every time.

I savor every second, every sensation.

I know she's not going to get all of me in, but damn I love that she is trying so hard. Still sucking my shaft, she cups my balls in one hand, rolling and firmly stroking them. My heart pounds like a drum, and my cock pulses hard. I'm dying to come, but I don't want this to be over yet. Hell, not ever.

My hips buck, and she lets me thrust into her mouth and throat. Her eyes roll up to find me watching as I fuck her mouth.

I lose it then. I can't take one second more.

"I'm gonna come..." I warn.

Her eyes are half-closed, sultry, as she carries on sucking up and down the length of me. I rear back and she sinks down one last time, taking me deep inside her throat.

With a roar of pleasure, I reach out and pinch her swollen nipples as the first spurts of my cum coat her tongue. While I shoot the rest of my load, her sapphire eyes never leave me. My thrusts into her slippery mouth slow, then still, and she swallows it all, every last drop. I stare down at her, at how beautiful she looks with my cock buried in her face. For the first time in my life, I have a strange thought: I never want this moment to end.

She carries on sucking gently.

God, what a woman.

RAINE

He pulls me up in one swift movement and whirls me around so my back is to the door.

"You drive me crazy," he groans, his hands sliding over my skin.

I lean my head against the door, moaning his name while his mouth skims my throat and his tongue darts out, hot and hungry. "Jesus, Raine," he rasps, his fingers digging into my ass.

My whimpers of pleasure echo around us as he caresses the curve of my ass, teasing both of us. He's right at the lacy hem of my soaked panties, stroking the sensitive skin. My fingers turn into claws as I grip his shoulders hard.

"Oh, my God," I moan as his mouth moves lower, and lower.

His tongue slides between my breasts, then he sucks and bites each nipple playing with it in his mouth until I want to scream. I hold his head close, urging him on, whispering his name over and over, while he grunts and grinds his rock-hard bulge against my belly. His tongue drags downwards and his fingers dip down there, between my thighs.

"Fuck, Raine, you're dripping onto my fingers," he growls when he feels how wet I am.

And now... he's on his knees. Sliding my panties down, he opens my legs wider. My head rolls from side to side when he buries his face between my legs. God, I'm in heaven. Fireworks explode behind my eyelids as I writhe and twist with pure ecstasy. His tongue sweeps up and down the length of my slit, lapping up my juices.

"You taste so sweet..." he mutters, before pushing his tongue deeper.

I gasp when he fucks me with his tongue. Suddenly, the tip of his tongue touches my aching, throbbing bundle of nerves, and my thighs clench, and to my total shock, an explosive orgasm rocks me to my core. He holds on to me tightly even as he continues to probe with his greedy tongue. All I know is, I'm floating in a delicious haze of pleasure, and I don't want to ever come back down to Earth.

When it is all over, and I'm panting hard, he stands and sweeps me up into his arms. Carrying me to the master bedroom he places me on the big bed. He peels off his shirt, revealing a body that looks like it was chiseled out of granite. In the soft light from the bedside lamp his skin looks warm, tanned, glistening. My fingers ache to touch him.

I need to feel his skin on mine. He practically tears my panties off my body, then stands looking down at me. In his eyes are naked hunger and possession. He is looking down at my body as if he owns it.

"Your body..." he whispers as he takes my breasts in his hands again. "Is unbelievable. I swear you are the sexiest woman I have ever met."

I drape my arms over his bare shoulders, pull him down on top of me, and relish the sensation of his hard, masculine body pressing into mine while we kiss and grind against each other. I never thought it could be like this, so exciting, so racy, and so, so hot. The tension in my body tightens with every kiss, every touch, every taste of his skin.

"I need you. Fuck, how I want you," he groans. His cock is hot and heavy against my skin.

"I want you too," I whisper back, my fingers close around his extraordinarily thick length. I feel as if I am not Raine Fillander, the girl from the poor side of town. I feel as if I am a powerful woman and he is my man. I know he is not really my man, but for this weekend he is. And that is all that counts. Even when my head may have denied it my body has wanted him from the moment I laid eyes on him and here I am... in his bed.

From the bedside table he takes a condom and quickly rolls it onto his dick. He guides his hardness to my entrance and gently pushes himself in. I gasp. He seems even bigger and thicker than I remember. Maybe it's because I'm still swollen from the last time he was inside me.

He kisses me softly, teasingly, and looks deep into my eyes as he pushes forward, watching my reaction as he slowly enters me inch by glorious inch, stretching me until I'm sure I can't take more, and yet there is more of him to go in.

"You okay?" he asks.

I nod. Already my body has adjusted.

He begins thrusting then, deep, sure thrusts. Again and again, until my eyes roll back in my head with the unbearable pleasure, and my mouth open to emit a cry of pure wonderment. I can't believe I am being so loud, but I can't be quiet.

True passion, true pleasure.

He rests on his forearms, and his weight feels heavy and welcome. I wrap my legs around him tightly and push my body upwards to drive him further inside me. I want all of him, always. Forever. Of course, that isn't possible, but I'm in a fantasy, a dream. And when you're dreaming everything is allowed. Even wishing this was for always.

Gently, I lick away the sweat from his throat and listen as he whispers my name against my neck. It's all so sweet, so impossibly perfect. Our bodies work together, moving as one, until we lose control and dissolve into frenzied bucking, crying out each time our bodies slam together.

"Yes!" I scream as I explode, my muscles clenching him like a fist.

I barely understand when he climaxes. I'm that far gone.

RAINE

I t is a crazy night. We hardly sleep. All night long we go at it. Even when we are so exhausted our eyes close without our knowledge, we sleep only fitfully, and reach for each other soon after. Until I do not know what is dreams of him and what we truly did. The room reeks of our lust.

Finally, when dawn is in the sky we fall into a deep sleep. I wake up to the feeling of a mouth between my legs. I widen my thighs and moan softly at the delicious heat of his tongue. Once I have climaxed he fills me all over again.

I watch him until he goes over the edge. It is beautiful to watch him lose control. To know I made that happen. To know right now, there is nothing else in his mind except me.

"Do you have a high-necked top?" he whispers in my ear.

I turn to look in his eyes. "Yes, but I might not wear it."

He smiles. "Good. You have exactly thirty minutes before your personal shopper arrives."

"Look, Konstantin. If it's all right with you. I really prefer not to shop. It's not that I'm not grateful to you for taking the trouble to arrange everything, but I'll feel better if I don't take advantage of your incredible generosity. For me you have already done more than I could ever have prayed for. It is enough."

"Nobody gave you the rule book, did they?"

"What rule book?"

"When you get invited to spend the weekend in London by a billionaire, the shopping trip is included in the deal. You don't get to refuse."

I bite my lip. "Are you always this generous?"

His answer is brief. "No."

"Then why now?"

"Because you need riding gear, something nice to wear to dinner this evening, and something very, very sexy that I can tear off your body tonight." He slaps my rump. "Now, off you go before I change my mind and fuck you again."

I jump out of bed laughing. Naked as the day I was born I head towards the door. There is more sway to my hips than normal. Let him watch and thirst. Then my foot steps on something next to his discarded jacket. I stop and pick it up. It is a USB stick. Holding it up I turn around.

"Is this what Lan—"

I stop abruptly because he has sat bolt upright in bed. That lazy indulgent expression in his eyes has completely disappeared and in its place a shocking intensity as his forefinger flies towards his mouth in a shhhh gesture.

He bounds out of bed, takes the stick from my hand and says, "Have a lovely time. I will explain when we get to my house this afternoon."

I stare at his intense face in shock. It is like stroking a tame cat and having it suddenly turn into a wild tiger. He presses my arm as if reassuring me, or just encouraging me to go along with whatever was going on. Shocked by the lightning fast change in him, and by the mystery of what is truly going on, I can only nod dumbly, and walk away towards the other bathroom, where all my toiletries still are.

As I shower I think about the USB stick and what could possibly be in it that is so secret it cannot even be spoken aloud about. Why did he silence even my innocent question? Does he think we are being surveilled? Is someone listening to us? What is he involved with?

By the time my hair is dried I am no wiser. As I pull my shoes on, the bell goes. I quickly rush out of the room and open the door. A small woman with a big smile is standing outside.

"Ah, you must be Raine. I'm Jane Barrymore, your stylist for the day."

"Hi, Jane. Er... come in. Would you like to have coffee or something?"

She glances at her watch. "No, I've had breakfast. I was thinking we could hit the shops running."

"Yeah, sure. Can we stop at a Starbucks or something?"

"Of course," she says with another massive smile.

For the next three hours we hit the shops, but shopping with Jane is a whole other experience. She takes me into air-conditioned, high-end boutiques where all the sales assistants look like perfectly made up dolls with attitude. But they fall over themselves to please her. In one place they even open a bottle of champagne for us.

I quickly realize that Jane's big, dopey smile is just a front. In fact, she is extremely efficient, professional, and exacting. She knows exactly what she wants and doesn't allow anybody to distract her with anything but exactly what she wants. If she wants an item in blue and they only have yellow, then she sends someone by taxi to another location to go fetch the color she wants. All right, or fine will not do. Only fabulous will.

My head is spinning with all the selections she makes me try on and discard. A trouser suit which I will never wear after this weekend, two silk blouses, a tight black skirt, an ephemerally beautiful blue dress that is exactly the same color as my eyes. A gorgeous baby blue summer coat for the warm evenings, and a riding habit. We also drop by a lingerie store where I pick up a couple of underwear sets, the sweetest gossamer pink nightie ever with matching suspenders and sheer white stockings.

Then she gets me a suitcase for me to transport all my new stuff back in. I don't know exactly how much money we have spent, but for sure it must have cost many thousands of pounds. Just the blue dress alone was £4,200,00. I saw the price tag before the sales assistant removed it.

"I think we're done," she declares looking at her small gold wrist watch. "And it is time for me to take you to Mr. Tsarnov."

I nod. "Right. Back to the hotel."

"No, actually. I believe you are having lunch at a restaurant and I'm supposed to drop you off outside."

"Oh."

We jump into the back of the car and her driver takes us back to Mayfair and comes to a stop in front of a restaurant called the Orange Bayleaf.

Jane turns to me. "There you are. Here is where I'm supposed to drop you off. Goodbye, Raine. I've really enjoyed our time together, and I know you are going to look stunning in everything we have selected."

I smile gratefully at her. "Thank you so much for your help. You were amazing. To be perfectly honest, I feel as if I've been in a whirlwind. Everything is moving so fast, but I have definitely enjoyed watching you work."

She flashes another of those disarming, big, artless smiles of hers. "Enjoy the rest of your stay in London, and if you are back here again, do give me a shout and we'll have coffee or something. My card will be delivered together with all your purchases directly to Mr. Tsarnov's driver at the hotel."

I thank her again and slip out of the car and walk towards the glass doors. On either side are huge pots of bamboo. My stomach is growling with hunger. Other than a yellow macaroon I was offered at one of the boutiques I haven't eaten anything since last night.

RAINE

I t is a terribly exclusive restaurant. You can feel it in the minimalist air. To start with there are more staff in starched, plain orange pinafores than there are patrons. The leaf green walls are without pictures or ornaments and the seats are black and yellow. Everything is either shining with polish or immaculately green.

A waiter comes to greet me.

I give him Konstantin's last name and he nods politely and takes me to a secluded table where Konstantin is seated. He is concentrating so hard on something on his ipad screen, he does not even realize I am there until I am almost on top of him. Still, it gives me a rare chance to study him while he is unaware and again I am struck by how different he is from any man I have ever gone out with. I remember the way he was when I accidentally found the USB stick.

"Hello," I whisper.

He looks up and smiles. The naked avenging god is gone. In its place the immaculately dressed, unknowable billionaire.

"Did you have a good time?"

"Yes, I did, thank you." I wrinkle my nose. "Jane is incredibly knowledgeable and easy going, but she has also railroaded me into buying a lot more stuff than I have ever bought in my life."

He grins. "Did you get something sexy for me to rip off?"

I giggle. "Yes."

He smiles, it carries promise and secrets. "Good."

The waiter comes and we order cocktails. The service is amazing and the drinks arrive almost immediately. My drink is sweet and refreshing. I sip it while I study the menu. It is a fusion restaurant, French and Thai. After we order we chat a bit about London.

The conversation is a surreal affair. He behaves as if nothing out of the ordinary has happened, but I cannot forget how quickly and frighteningly intense his eyes became in a fraction of a second. There is more, much more to him than he shows the world.

What secret is he hiding? He said he would tell me when we get to his house and I will just have to be patient until then.

The food arrives quickly. Since the establishment bears all the marks of a pretentious nouvelle cuisine restaurant, I expected the overpriced food to come in tiny portions with weird tasting ingredients, but I am surprised by how totally yummy my pickled green papaya and smoked duck are. And they are not small either.

I lean back on the chair replete. "What's next on the agenda?"

"I believe you wanted a ride on an open-top bus, didn't you?"

"Yeah, but I don't really want to go on my own so I've given up on the idea. If I come back I'll do it."

"I'm coming with you."

My eyes widen with surprise. "You'll come with me on a bus?"

"Well, sort of."

"What does that mean?"

"Come, I'll show you." We walk out of the door, cross the road and go into the building opposite. A man sitting at the reception nods respectfully at him. There is an elevator at the foyer which we enter.

"Where are we going?" I ask.

"Patience, Raine," he teases.

The elevator doors swish open and we get out to a narrow space with a set of stairs. We walk up the stairs together, he opens a fire door and I step out onto the roof of the building. There is a helicopter waiting on a helipad.

"We're going in that?" I scream, my voice full of excitement.

He smiles at me, a smile of indulgence and pleasure, like a father who presents his daughter with her first bicycle. "Yes."

"Wow, This is so ah-ma-zing," I gush.

Then the pilot starts the chopper's engine, the blades start moving, wind whips my hair into my face and eyes, and the air fills with the sound of the engine. With a laugh of pure joy, I tuck my head down, and hand in hand we run towards the chopper like children on the way to a fabulous adventure.

The trip is the best thing that has ever happened in my life, oh wait, after the sex that is. The sex with Konstantin Tsarnov is obviously and definitely the best, but this is a close second.

RAINE

By the time we arrive back at the hotel my body is pulsing for him. The need is so powerful I can hardly keep my hands off him in the old-fashioned elevator. As soon as we get to the suite, he slams the door with his foot and crushes me to him. I wrap my arms around him.

"What do you want me to do to you?" he asks, his voice deep and hungry in my ear.

My mind spins with the possibilities. I don't even know where to start. "Anything," I breathe.

He cups my pussy with the palm of his hand. I moan and try to grind down against him, to find some kind of relief, but he moves his hand away. He wants me to suffer. And I *am* suffering. Then he scoops me into his arms and strides to the bed, where he drops me unceremoniously, then starts pulling all my clothes off. First my jeans get yanked off, then my blouse is ripped open so roughly, buttons fly off. My bra offers no resistance and the slip of lace covering my sex tears away easily. Stark naked I stare up at him. Wanting whatever he wants. Ready for whatever he plans to do to me.

He grabs my ankles and opens my legs wide.

"Fuck, you're so wet," he growls, as if looking at my wet pussy is driving him crazy. "But I'm going to make you drip even more. Get on your hands and knees."

I obey instantly, my palms spread out on the cool bed sheets, my ass facing him.

I feel his warm hands on my ass cheeks. Slowly he spreads them, letting out a soft groan as he does so. "Fuck, you look good like this."

Knowing how much just the sight of my ass is turning him on sends another surge of desire through my body. My pussy aches for attention. I feel his hot breath on my virgin ass, and then, he leans forward and licks my ass.

"Oh God..." I groan loudly. This is so damn hot.

"You are so fucking sexy, so fucking sexy," he murmurs, his breath warm against my skin.

He flicks his tongue around me, moving slow; his tongue is warm and soft. He slides a hand under my stomach and, holding me in place, moves his other hand between my legs. He finds my clit and presses his flattened fingers lightly on my painfully over sensitized clitoris and starts massaging me softly.

My mouth drops open and my hands clench the sheets.

Holy shit. I'm still struggling to believe that this is really happening to me. I feel as if I am going to shatter.

"Oh yes," I gasp.

"You know tonight, I'm going to fill this ass with my cock, don't you?" he whispers.

"Yes," I groan, as my pussy juices drip down my thighs.

He dives back in, licking and probing me gently with his tongue like he can't get enough of me. I give up trying to do anything but enjoy this... this experience. Wow, he's so *good* at this. He massages my clit a little harder than before, and I let out a loud, guttural groan of pleasure, and he attacks me with more intent than before, reacting to me, responding to how much I love his mouth on me. I'm so close to climax.

"Are you going to come for me?" he asks.

"Yes, yes," I gasp, grinding myself frantically against his hand. He sinks his fingers into my pussy and that's all I need to push me over the edge.

"Fuck!" I cry, the word bursting forth from me before I can stop it. Not that I want to. My pussy clenches hard and my back arches as my orgasm tears through me.

He drags his large hands down my sides and, cupping my breasts, tweaks the nipples between his thumb and forefinger, then pinches them. Hard. That draws a gasp from between my lips.

"I need to fuck you," he says suddenly, his voice thick with lust.

He strips quickly and while he grabs a condom from the bedside table and rolls it onto him, I check out his gorgeous body. I gaze hungrily at his muscles perfectly sculpted. His body is taut and lean where mine is soft and full of curves.

He grabs my hips and I feel his cock head pushing up against the entrance of my wet, ready slit. Part of me wants him to slam the thick shaft into me. But another part of me wants to take my time, make this slow, savor every second.

His big cock stretches and fills me. It feels amazing. I know, I am forever ruined for any other man. I turn slightly to look at him and he is gritting his teeth, like he's trying to keep from coming right then and there. I love the effect I have on him. There's something intoxicating about knowing that he's so into me he has to fight not to lose control.

"You look fucking incredible," he growls, as he begins to slam into me.

His thrusts are so strong I have to clench the sheets so I don't get thrown across the bed. His cock is deeper in me than it ever has been before.

I press against him to take him even deeper. He tips his head back, jaw clenching once more. I can tell he's getting close.

I don't take my eyes from his face. I want to see this, to watch him give in to how much he wants me. I feel my pussy clenching once more, tightening around his cock, and to my surprise realize that I, too, am close again. I reach up and run my hands over his body, forcing myself to remember this moment, this feeling.

"Fuck ..." He roars as he thrusts himself into me, deep and hard, one last time.

He comes hard, his body shaking, and moments later I follow him into the abyss, every inch of me trembling with pleasure as my second orgasm explodes in me.

He slowly pulls out and disposes of the condom, before crashing back down on the bed next to me.

"Now come sit on my face," he orders.

I hesitate for a second, surprised that he wouldn't want to rest for a bit then, dizzy with lust, I crawl up to his face and put my wet, swollen pussy on his hot mouth.

And all thoughts of visiting the Tower of London and the Dungeon are forgotten.

Gone.

Obliterated.

Kaput.

RAINE

I see the creatures after we drive into the long driveway of Huntington Manor. They are quite a distance away and they are peacefully grazing. At first I think I must be dreaming because they are like something from a fairytale. Two horses, one pure gold and another the color of champagne, but in the evening light they are glowing as if they are made from burnished metal, and yet, they are moving and moving so fluidly and elegantly, they cannot possibly be mechanical horses.

"Wow! Are those special horses? I have never seen anything like them before."

"They are a wild Turkmen horse breed. They're called Akhal-Teke, but because of their shiny coats they are more often referred to as Golden Horses."

"They are tame. Can I ride one of them?"

"Those two are not suitable for you, but I have a placid mare that you will love."

I turn to look at him. "What makes you think I need a placid mare?"

He holds his hands up. "Don't bite my head off. I'd just rather be safe than sorry."

"I'll have you know when I was a kid I used to ride a horse without a saddle."

He laughs. "Somehow I can imagine that."

Then the car pulls up to a massive house made of gray and white stone. Six thick, tall Greek style pillars adorn the front of the house. A man dressed like a traditional butler is already waiting at the top of the stairs. He looks the way I have always imagined a butler would. He has expressive, pale blue eyes, and to my amusement even his name is James.

He greets us with warm, lemon scented towels. He tells us there is a jug of Pimms and fruit waiting for us on the South terrace. Konstantin thanks him, then sends him away on an errand, and we are alone again.

"Wow, the way you live," I whisper.

"Do you have your cellphone on you?"

"Yes."

He takes a pen out of his jacket pocket and drops it on the stone floor.

"What are you doing?' I ask confused.

"Can you unlock your phone and give it to me?"

I'm surprised, but I take my phone out of my purse and hand it over to him. He takes it from me and I see his fingers move with lightning speed on my screen. Then he hands the phone back to me.

"Read it," he instructs.

I start reading and a frown appears on my face. I look up at him. "What is going on?"

"Continue reading," he says softly.

So I continue reading. I am reading the exact transcript of our conversation. I scroll upwards and everything we said in the car is there. The transcript actually ends with the sentence that actually makes my skin crawl.

Pen drops on hard floor.

I look up at him. "What is this?"

He shrugs. "Your phone is listening to you. Everything you say and what others say in your presence is recorded forever. It's all there if you know how to look for it."

I gaze at him in confusion. "I don't understand. Are you saying somebody has tapped my phone?"

"No, everyone's smart phone is recording them twenty-four seven."

"But how did it know that you dropped a pen on a hard floor?" I ask still in disbelief.

"The AI has accumulated so much data and become so advanced it is now able to distinguish the different sounds."

I take a deep breath. Wow, I will never feel the same about my phone again. It is not just tracking my location, which I knew about and dismissed as a necessary evil, but its actually spying on my private life. "Why did you show me this?"

"Because I'm going to have to ask you to put your phone into a Faraday cage while you remain in this house."

"Oh, but I'm expecting my mom to Skype me."

"We have landline telephones in many parts of the house and a computer room if you prefer to speak on video chat."

Silently, I hand the phone to him. We go into the foyer and it is made of pure white marble. It is breathtakingly beautiful. The graceful curved staircase has a deep red runner carpet. He puts both our phones into a metal cabinet hidden away inside an antique mini cupboard.

"Tell me about the USB stick Lana gave you," I say.

"I cannot tell you anything about that, Raine. It is a secret project. In fact, I would have preferred it if you had not seen the stick at all. The less you know the safer it is for you."

I nod. "Okay, I understand. Let's just say I never saw anything."

He smiles slowly. "Thank you. One day I will tell you."

I smile back. I think I'm falling for this guy. He is everything I dreamed about in a man.

"Shall we go have a drink on the terrace?"

He holds out his elbow and I slip my hand through it.

"After our drink I need to make some calls so you can roam the house or take a walk on the grounds. It is very beautiful at this time of the year. And after that you are learning to drive my lambo."

"What?" I splutter.

He looks down at me, an amused quirk to his mouth. "Don't you want to?"

"Hell, yeah."

RAINE

I f Konstantin thought I was going to be afraid of driving his matt black Lamborghini he had another think coming. I stepped on the gas and gave him the shock of his life. I had to laugh at his expression. I'm not afraid of big monster vehicles. When I was twelve my granddad let me drive his tractor. Once I knew pressing the button lightly kept the car running at a subtle noise decibel, but pressing it hard made the car roar like a beast. I pressed it hard and went screaming down all kinds of country lanes.

When we stopped at a deserted field, he pulled me out of the car and couldn't wait to have his way with me. I will never again look at the image of an English countryside without feeling the grass on my knees and palms, my eyes turned up towards a clear blue sky, the sound of crows cawing in the distance, the smell of hot soil in my nose, and Konstantin's hand pulling my hair, and his hard, hot cock thrusting urgently into my body. Again and again and again.

That was two hours ago. Now I stand in front of the mirror in my beautiful new blue dress. Gingerly, I touch a tendril of hair that has already escaped the complicated French plait that I unsuccessfully tried to put it into.

With a sigh I pull the whole thing down, brush it all out, then make my way down the stairs. I do not know where Konstantin's room is. I am in a very feminine guest bedroom decorated in shades of cream and rose.

As I walk down the red runner carpet I wonder about Konstantin. He seems to need his space and privacy. Even at the hotel, it was perfectly clear even though he never said it aloud, that we both had separate rooms, separate bathrooms.

I wander into the truly massive living room. The ceilings are at least twenty feet high and the walls are thick and intricately carved. There are two large fireplaces. A grand piano sits in one end of the room. It faces tall windows that look onto acres of green landscape. For someone who lives in New York it is a truly unusual sight. I grew up on a farm but the grass was never this green.

Konstantin has not come down yet and I walk over to the open doors. Evening sunlight touches my skin, warming me. I hear a sound behind me and turn.

Konstantin stops walking and stares at me.

"What is it?"

"Wow, you look amazing standing there in the sunlight." He comes closer and touches my hair. "Your hair is like gold. You looked like an angel just now."

I lick my bottom lip.

He reaches out a hand and touches it. "I'm invited to a pool party at the home of the Crown Prince of UAE. Do you want to go see how the truly rich party, or do you want to stay and have dinner here?"

"Stay and have dinner here with you," I say immediately.

"It'll be something you've never done before."

"Staying here and having dinner with you will be something I've never done before."

"Okay. We'll go to bed early. I like to ride before the sun gets too hot."

"Yeah, let's go to bed like really early," I say with a grin.

"Your eyes are amazing. So blue... like wet jewels," he says softly.

"I was thinking the same thing about yours," I tease.

James appears with a tray of two champagne glasses. He withdraws as unobtrusively as he arrived. We sit in the light from the dying sun, drink our champagne and talk.

"So... how does a self-confessed nerd become a billionaire?"

He leans back and closes his eyes. "I'm a hacker and a coder. A very brilliant hacker and coder. I put together a currency platform that's worth billions."

"I saw the photo of you and Putin. Is he your friend?"

He opens his eyes and looks at me. "Look, Raine. I don't want to talk to you about my work. I want to keep you protected. The less you know the safer you will be."

I swallow the mouthful of champagne, and mumble, "Okay. I understand."

"Tell me about you?" he invites.

So I tell him about my life, the two jobs, my mother, my sister, the apartment we live in, the gratitude we feel because my sister is still alive. He asks about my childhood and my voice becomes far away and distant when I remember how happy our lives were, while my father was still alive. We had prize winning goats, hens, a cow and some pigs. My mother grew her own vegetables and my father cultivated corn. We went to bed early and were up at the crack of dawn, and we worked all the hours that God sent. There was so much to do, but the air was clean, we kept close bonds with the rest of the farming community, and we were always happy.

He leans forward eagerly. "Tell me more about this farm. What kinds of things did you do?"

"Well, I was in charge of the hens," I say. "I fed them, I cleaned out their houses, and I collected their eggs. They were like my pets. I would squat in the dirt and open my arms and they would come running into them. They were so sweet. I loved them so much so I fought my parents and never allowed any of them to end up on our dinner table, but when we left we had to sell them all to a neighbor. They eat their chickens."

A sigh escapes me. I haven't spoken to anyone about them ever since we left and I feel a sense of nostalgia and sadness for my little friends. For that simple, happy life we left behind.

"Why did you come to New York?" His voice is soft in the cool evening air. The sun has already set.

I exhale the breath I was holding. "My mother's sister was living there then and she told us to come and live with her. The Big Apple. Where the streets are paved with gold. What a shock my mother got when we arrived. Sometimes I feel we would have been better off on the farm, but we'll never know."

James comes to tell us dinner is ready to be served, and we move to the great dining room, our bodies touching. There is a closeness between us that wasn't there before. I slant a glance at him. His face is closed, but I know something has changed in him. Something is different.

The dining table has been set for two. It's clear the room is hardly ever used as our voices echo in the still air. I look around me. It feels as if I am living in a fairytale. Those horses, the land, the house, this candlelit room. I feel like Bella from Beauty and the Beast, only in my case, my beast has already been turned into a Prince.

Waiting staff come into the room. They fill the glasses in front of us with water and wine. The wine is cool and complicated. I'm not a wine person, but I like this wine.

"The wine is lovely," I murmur.

"Yes, I have a sommelier who fills my cellar."

"Wow, what a life you lead."

"Actually, most of the time, I am working."

"Do you ever get lonely, Konstantin?"

"No," he denies instantly, then he pauses. "My work is very important to me."

"Don't you ever want to settle down, have a family?"

He looks away from me. "Yes, one day. But not now. I have to do this thing first. It is very important."

"It's the secret project you're working on, isn't it?"

"Yes." And then he changes the subject. So we start talking about horses and then he invites me to go sailing in the Mediterranean with him. I feel pleasure surge into my body as I stare at him in astonishment. It's just a small thing and it probably doesn't mean anything, maybe he does this all the time, but he wants to see me again after the weekend.

I am so incredibly happy I can hardly eat. I finally understand what people mean when they say, I'm on cloud nine.

RAINE

I think I might have drunk too much, because the rest of the night passes in a dream. We touch, we kiss, we hold, and we have sex, but sex feels different. It feels as if he cares. Of course, I don't fool myself that he really does, but it just feels as if he does. It's probably all that alcohol sloshing around in my veins.

We wake up early in the morning and I go to my room and slip into my new riding gear, complete with riding boots and go outside. The air is crisp. He is standing next to a pillar looking into the distance. He seems to be lost in deep thought.

"Hey," I whisper.

He whirls around to look at me. "Wow! Turn around."

I obey.

"You have the sexiest ass I've ever seen," he decides.

I blush. I don't know why I'm blushing.

He smiles, a knowing smile. I look at his beautiful face and start to feel butterflies fluttering in my tummy. But I don't want to be like Chloe and the girl who tried to throw herself off the building. I need to keep myself sane. I need to keep a little bit of myself aloof. This is just a dream. When it is over he will be gone and I will have a healthy sister.

We ride together. Konstantin on a shiny black Arabian stallion, and me on a beautiful golden horse called Laika. It was immediate when I sat astride her that riding a horse is like riding a bicycle. You never forget. Laika responds beautifully. I pat her shiny neck.

"Shall we race that silly black Arabian stallion?"

She moves her head as if nodding.

"Wanna race?"

Konstantin's eyebrows rise. "Why? You feel like losing?"

"Are you too chicken?"

He laughs. "No, I just like to have you in one piece."

I laugh. "Oh, you little coward."

"Go on. I'll give you a head start."

"No, I don't want a head start. I want to win fair and square."

"You know, I don't think I've ever met a woman like you."

"I don't think I've ever met a man like you either. Now, are we racing or not?"

He grins. "On the count of three?"

"On the count of three," I confirm.

Of course, I lose. It's not Laika's fault. No one told me that the Arabian stallion could actually fly.

To his credit, he doesn't gloat. We go back and have a huge English breakfast. I have the works. Fried tomatoes, sausages, bacon, eggs, baked beans, and mushrooms. I don't know whether it's how this produce tastes in England or it could be the fresh air and the exercise, but it all tastes absolutely delicious.

Then it is time for us to leave. As I pack my suitcase, I actually shed some tears. What if I never come back? I have so loved my time in London.

The trip back passes too quickly. Yes, we have sex, but it feels too quickly over. I feel almost tearful, but I remind myself no one likes a clingy tearful woman. I won't be like Chloe and the other girl. I won't do that to myself or him.

There is a separate car waiting for me.

"I'll call you," he says, as he bundles me into it.

"Okay," I croak. Then the door is shut and the car moves away. I turn my head to watch him. He lifts his hand in a wave and I wave back. Then I turn my head forward and stare at the leather upholstery in the car. I won't cry. I just won't cry. I will concentrate on only one thing. I have saved my sister.

The driver drops me off outside my house. He helps me with my suitcases. "It's okay. I can manage from here," I tell him.

"You sure?" he asks. "I don't mind taking them to your door.

"It's okay, thanks."

I wheel my two suitcases into the lift. I feel strangely light-headed. I cannot believe how much I miss him. The lift opens and I get in. Tears fill my eyes. I dash them away. Stop being so silly. Grow up for God's sake. It was just a dirty weekend. As long as Maddy gets her treatment, and I instinctively know he won't break his word, then nothing else matters.

I get out of the elevator and head towards our home. For the first time, I notice how shabby the corridor is. The peeling paint, the threadbare carpet, the stains. I put my key in the door and the door gets yanked open.

Maddy throws her arms around me. "I've missed you," she cries passionately.

"Hey, hey, what's going on here? I've only been gone for a weekend."

"It feels like forever," she complains. "Don't go away again, please."

"Oh Maddy, Maddy, Maddy."

"I had a bad dream about you," she whispers in my ear. "I dreamed your plane crashed."

"Your dreams are nonsensical," I say with a laugh.

"I thought you died."

I pull away from her and smile. "Me? Died? Never."

My phone starts ringing. I pull it out of my purse thinking it is Konstantin. But it is not. It is Catherine Moriarty.

RAINE

I untangle myself from my sister. My heart is beating so fast I am afraid Maddy will hear it.

"Hello, Catherine," I say as calmly as I can. I know my sister is watching.

"You have not done the job you were paid to do," Catherine says. Her voice is cold as ice.

"I need to talk to you."

"What about?"

"Um, can we meet?"

"At the coffee place down the road from you in one hour?"

"The Breadstick?"

"Yes."

"Yes, that would be fine."

Then the line goes dead. I stare at the phone.

"Who the hell was that?" Maddy asks.

"Just work. A difficult customer," I lie.

"Oh, now tell me all about your dirty weekend in London."

"Do you mind if I get through the door first, young lady?"

She moves back and catches sight of my new suitcase. "Ooooo, what's that? A new suitcase?"

"Yes, I say wheeling both my suitcases through the door and shutting it."

"What's in the suitcase?" Maddy asks curiously.

I love Maddy with all my heart, but right at that moment my head feels like it is spinning. I am dizzy with anxiety. Catherine was clearly furious with me, and telling her I'm not going to switch the painting is not going to be a fun experience.

"What's in the suitcase?" Maddy asks again.

"I did some shopping," I say looking down at the suitcases blankly. There is a horrible feeling in my stomach.

"You mean the billionaire took you shopping?"

I turn to look at her, her eyes are round with astonishment and curiosity. "No, he arranged for me to shop with a personal stylist."

"Oh my God! That is just like a romance movie. Shall I make us some coffee and you can tell me everything?"

"Maddy, I can't talk now. I have to meet that person who just called. It won't be a good meeting because I didn't do what I was supposed to. So I'm just going to go to my room and prepare myself for a bit, okay. We'll talk tonight."

Her shoulders slump and she looks defeated. "Okay."

I hate to see her like that. "Chin up, pumpkin. We'll talk when I come back, all right."

"All right."

I turn to go.

"Raine?

I turn back. "Yeah?"

"I missed you."

"Come here," I say, opening my arms.

She rushes into them and I hug her thin body tightly. "I have so much to tell you and I also bought you a present, but just let me get past this difficult meeting, okay?"

I open my arms and she moves back. "Good luck with your meeting."

"Thank you."

I go to my room and I sit on my bed. I stare at the wall and rehearse what I am going to tell Catherine. When I have it all pat, I stand and walk to the door. Maddy is staring into her cellphone, and she does not even realize I have come into the living room. She looks almost hypnotized by the flickering light coming from it.

"I am going out now, Maddy."

She jerks her head up. "Okay, see you soon. Don't let her push you around."

I smile. "See you soon."

I take my time walking down the sidewalk. I breathe evenly and deeply. A vagrant is going through trash. He finds a half-eaten sandwich and starts eating it. No matter how many times I see it, the sight always saddens me. People are not meant to live in cities. All of us scurrying about like rats. It's not right.

As I reach the café, I straighten my spine, square my shoulder and approach, keeping myself as calm as possible.

Even though I am ten minutes early, Catherine is already there, which for some reason gives her a psychological advantage. There is a glass of water in front of her.

"Sit down," she says, her face is cold and hard. Strange, but she even seems like a different person.

I slip into the seat opposite her.

"Why haven't you switched the painting yet?"

"Look, I'm sorry, but I can't do it. I feel too guilty. I'm just going to return the money that you have wired into my bank account and let's just call it quits."

She shakes her head. "Let's just call it quits." She starts laughing, then shakes her head again. "It's not often I am wrong, but when I am wrong I can be spectacularly wrong. I thought you were a smart cookie. Looks like you're the dumbest broad in New York. You can't give the money back. This operation has cost hundreds of thousands of dollars. All the other girls have been paid. I have been paid for my time. And if you can pay all those people and for all the time spent to set up this job it still won't be enough because these people don't want the money back. They want the painting switched."

"Why is the painting so important to your clients?"

She leans forward, her eyes glittering with emotion. "That's none of your business. Your job is simple. All you have to do is to switch the painting and then nothing more will be asked of you."

"Isn't there another way?"

"No, there is no other way. Try to see it from their point of view. If you had not taken this job, then another girl would have been picked and the painting would have been switched by now. You've ruined the perfect set up. Something that took many, many months and hundreds of thousands of dollars to arrange."

"I know I messed up, and I'm really, really sorry, but I just can't do it. The only thing I can do is slowly pay back all the money that your clients have spent and they will just have to find another way to get the painting they want."

She sighs. "I don't think you get it. You cannot walk away from a job like this just because you decide that you like riding the mark's dick. Once you're in you're in... or there will be consequences to pay."

"Consequences?" I whisper.

"Yes, consequences. These people have no limits. If you cross them they will come for your family. I hope you understand Raine what I mean when I say that. Your mother... or even your sick little sister."

I freeze with fear. My mind is unable to assimilate the knowledge that they know everything about me and my family.

"They won't stop until you do what they want you to. Do you really want to risk your family for a stupid painting or for a man you mean nothing to?"

I swallow hard. I can almost feel all the little bones in Maddy's thin body pressing into my flesh.

"This is the skull at your banquet that cannot be denied," Catherine says.

I stare down at the table surface. At that moment a waitress appears on my right. "What can I get you?" she asks.

I look up at her. She has bright red hair, tattoos on her neck, and a nose ring. I shake my head. "Nothing, thank you. I'm leaving."

She nods and flounces away.

I turn back to Catherine. "All right, I'll do it."

She smiles, but it doesn't reach her eyes. "When can you do it?"

"I'll try to do it tomorrow."

"Good. Call me after you have done it."

I nod.

"You can go now."

I stand like a robot and walk out of the café. I feel as if I am in a daze. My dream has just turned into a horrific nightmare.

RAINE

I walk aimlessly for a long time. Sometimes people tut at me. I seem to be in their way. They are in a rush to get somewhere. My mother texts me to know where I am. I tell her not to worry. Everything is fine. I will be along soon.

I walk until it suddenly becomes clear in my head. And I know exactly what to do about it as well.

Maddy is in bed and my mother is back by the time I arrive home. As I close the front door, she walks out of the kitchen while wiping her hands on a towel.

"What's going on?" she asks, a worried frown on her face.

"Come and sit down, Mom." She sits on the old sofa and I join her. And I'm about to tell her when I suddenly remember the phone in my pocket, all the phones in our house. We are literally surrounded by listening devices.

"Wait. Can we take a walk outside and I'll tell you everything then?"

"Walk? Why? I just got home after a very long day at work, Raine. I'm exhausted. Can you tell me here?"

"No, Mom. I'm sorry, but this is important."

She stands and walks towards her coat. Shrugging into it, she says, "Come on then."

"Mom, have you got your cell phone on you?"

"Yes, it's in my coat."

I walk towards her, putting my forefinger over my lips to warn her not to speak, I take the phone out of her coat and leave it on the table together with mine.

Then we walk out of the apartment. As soon as we reach the street, she turns towards me. "What on earth is going on?"

"Mom, I think I'm in trouble. I think I've accidentally got mixed up with some very bad people."

My mother pales, her hand rushes to her mouth. "What's happening, Raine?"

"You know that painting that I was supposed to switch because it has sentimental value to someone. I don't think that's true. I think I was desperate for money, I deliberately fooled myself. I let myself believe such an obvious lie. Who would go to all the trouble they went to just to get back a valueless painting? I think that painting has a listening device in it. I think someone is trying to bring Konstantin down."

"Don't do it, Raine. Give the money back," Mom bursts out instantly.

"They won't let me give them the money back. I have to do it, or they will hurt you or Maddy."

"Oh God!" Her eyes are filled with horror. "We have to go to the police."

"Mom, remember what Catherine told me at the beginning. They have bought the police and even the judges. We would be signing our death warrants if we do that. We cannot take on people like these. They are criminals, but they are very powerful and roam in a world we know nothing of."

"Should we pack our bags and leave the city?"

"No. We can't do that. That will mean Maddy will die in the next year."

Tears fill my mother's eyes. "What do we do then?"

"Tomorrow I will somehow arrange to go to Konstantin and I will switch the painting. Once I have done that I will pretend to him that I want to redecorate his office. I will tell him it has always been a dream of mine to try out some interior design and why not his office. I know he doesn't care anything about décor so he will probably say yes if I push. If he says yes, I will get some workmen in and get them to move the painting to another room. An unused room. They cannot blame me if they think the redecoration was planned a long time ago and I had nothing to do with it. And I'm going to close my bank account tomorrow so they can't deposit their dirty money into it anymore. Whatever is in it now, I'm going to donate to the homeless charity down the road."

"What if Konstantin says no?"

"I don't think he will say no, but if he does then I will cross that bridge when I come to it."

"How did this happen to us?"

"It's my fault, Mom. I was careless, but I promise I am going to make it alright. I am going to save Maddy, and I'm not going to let those people destroy Konstantin."

"How are you going to save Maddy if you're giving back all the money or giving it to charity?"

"Konstantin promised to pay for all Maddy's treatment. Not only that he wants us to do it here, at the best hospital, with the best doctors at whatever the cost."

My mother gasps. "He promised?"

"He promised."

"You believe him?"

"I believe him," I say softly, very firmly.

My mother grabs me into a big bear hug and begins to sob into my shoulder.

"It's okay, Mom. Everything is going to be okay. You'll see. I'll make it okay."

RAINE

Konstantin is as good as his word. While I am at work I receive a text from my mother that his secretary called to say she will be making arrangements for Maddy's treatment. I put my phone down wearing a huge smile and get back to my boring, mindless job of making sure two columns of numbers marry up.

An hour later my phone pings with a text.

> Him: *Want to have dinner with me tonight?*
> Me: *Would totally love to. Where are we going?*
> Him: *My place*
> Me: *Great. What time?*
> Him: *Car will come for you at 8.00pm*

I feel sad as I type out the next words. I'm going to betray him. I am the Judas, biting the hand that is saving my sister's life.

> Me: *I can't wait. Xx*

Him: *Wear that sexy thing you bought in London.*
Me: *Aye, Aye, Captain.*

There is no reply to that, and I stare at the wall in front of me despondently. I don't know how I am going to persuade him to let me redecorate his office, but I must.

"Have you finished that last batch?" my supervisor asks.

"Uh... nearly.

"Upstairs needs it urgently."

"Right. On it." I get back to work and put my troubles away until 8.00 pm tonight.

❄

*K*onstantin's place is on West End Avenue in the Beaux Arts landmark condominium. The lobby is accessed from a quiet, tree and brownstone-lined block just around the corner from Riverside Park. I have never been to this area of the city, and it is rather beautiful, but I can't appreciate any of it.

My stomach is tied up in knots and I feel as nervous and restless as a cat on a hot tin roof.

A smiling, middle-aged woman lets me into his home, a spectacular combination of two penthouses, a solarium penthouse and a terrace penthouse and set on two floors. My phone is put away into a similar contraption as the one he had in Berkshire.

Then I am led into the room that the floorplan I was given by Catherine called the great big room relates. Calling it a great big room was no exaggeration. It has a barrel-vaulted ceiling with a magnificent skylight that must be at least twenty-two-foot tall. There are full arched glass walls and French doors that lead to a terrace. It must look amazing during the day with sunlight pouring into it.

"This way please. Mr. Tsarnov is waiting outside for you," she says, walking towards the French doors.

Stunned by the beauty of his home, I follow wordlessly. The amount of outdoor space he has is shocking by this city's standards.

"Hello," Konstantin says softly. He is leaning against the railing.

"Hello," I say standing awkwardly on the gold-marble floors. I hear the woman withdrawing quietly back into the house.

"Come and have a drink," he invites.

I walk over to a low table where a bottle of champagne is sitting in an ice bucket. He pours us a glass each.

"Is everything alright?" he asks, a slight frown on his forehead.

I clutch my purse and try to sound normal. "Yes. Yes, everything is fine. I didn't know we wouldn't be alone."

He looks at me quizzically. "My housekeeper is leaving. She only stayed to cook our meal."

I sigh internally with relief. There is no way I can slip into his office if she is in the kitchen as I would have to pass the kitchen to get to his office. I put my purse on the low table.

"Oh, I see," I murmur.

As if on cue his housekeeper appears at the edge of the terrace. "If you don't need anything else, I'll be going now, Mr. T."

"Yes, you can go now. Goodnight, Mary."

I take a gulp of champagne and wander over to the railing. The river views are breathtaking. I turn back and find him watching me. A light breeze ruffles his hair. I stare at him. My heart feels heavy. I don't want to betray him, not even for a day, but I have no choice. I cannot risk those criminals hurting my sister or my mother.

What else can I do? I'll make the exchange today, then I'll keep him occupied all night and tomorrow I will arrange for the painting to be moved, before any damage can be done. Even so, I feel horribly guilty.

"What's the matter, Raine?" His voice is soft, but insistent.

"I'm just a little nervous, I guess. Everything we did before felt like a dream. This feels real."

He walks to me and pulls me towards him, molding my body to his. "No, it still feels like a dream," he whispers.

I nearly cry. I feel terrible. I'm going to betray him. "Oh, Konstantin," I gasp.

Then he kisses me. God, he tastes so good. The glass of champagne in my hand falls to the ground and shatters, but I don't hear it. Neither of us stops. I kiss him back with a desperation that is shocking. Almost as if I want to be sucked into him and disappear. Become part of him so I don't need to betray him. He moves his mouth away and begins to kiss my neck. I moan softly.

"Fuck, you're like a drug," he mutters. Then he scoops me into his arms and carries me to his bedroom.

It is a relief. It is a relief to stop thinking. To stop feeling like I sold out the only man who's shown me nothing but kindness for thirty pieces of silver.

RAINE

I sit on a stool in his shirt and watch as he stirs the pot of Bolognese sauce Mary prepared earlier in a kitchen that is equipped for serious cooking. It has a Sub-Zero fridge, a vented Wolf 48-inch dual fuel stove, two dishwashers, warming drawers, a pot filler and a butler's pantry.

"I never thought of you as a Bolognese person," I tease.

"What are you talking about? It may not be Russian cuisine but nonetheless I love Bolognese. Don't forget I was poor longer than I've been rich. I used to live in a tiny room and all I had was an electric hot plate. Spaghetti Bolognese was a treat. Every Saturday was Bolognese night."

"I can't imagine you as a nerd or poor."

He sticks some spaghetti into the boiling water. "You don't have to imagine it. I have pictures."

"Let's have a look then."

"I have to dig them out from the spare room upstairs."

"Oh please. Can I see them now?"

His eyebrows rise. "Now?"

"Yes, I'd absolutely love to see them. The spaghetti needs at least ten minutes. Come on."

"All right," he says, as he moves away from the stove.

As soon as I hear him reach the top of the stairs I fly in my bare feet to the terrace and grab my purse. My heart is racing so hard in my chest I can hear my blood rushing in my ears. I run to his office. Please, please, don't let the door be locked, I pray silently.

The door isn't.

I see the painting instantly. My hands are shaking, but switching it over is easy. As quickly as I came in, I leave and run back out to the terrace. I put my purse back on the table and run back to the kitchen where I take my place at the kitchen island once more. I flick my hair and adjust my shirt and try to control my quick breathing.

I'm almost in a state of disbelief.

The switch is done!

I can hardly believe that I've actually done it.

I hear a sound and I turn. Konstantin comes in carrying an iPad. He puts it in front of me and goes to the stove. I look down at the screen and for a moment I don't see anything. Everything just looks like pixels. I blink a few times and my vision clears. I stare down at the young man in the pictures.

"Believe me now?" he asks.

I look up at him. My god, I've just betrayed him, but I'm falling in love with him. I force a smile and keep my voice light. "You obviously have no idea what a nerd looks like. Think Bill Gates, Mark Zuckerberg or that Jeff Bezos before he got all pumped out on steroids."

He grins. "I was thinking of them."

"Then you're blind," I shoot back.

"He drains the pasta, pulls the plates from the warmer, and expertly coils the spaghetti onto the plates. Then he spoons the sauce on top, and brings the steaming plates over to me. The food is good, but I find it hard to swallow anything. When the meal is over he asks if I want some tiramisu, but I tell him I am too full to eat another thing. I make up a story about how I overate during lunch.

"Hey, how about giving me a tour of the place?"

"Sure."

His penthouse is absolutely beautiful, there is no other way to describe it. I start to doubt my plan of wanting to redecorate his apartment. When we get to his office door, he pushes it open and says, "And this is my office where I spend a huge amount of time."

I stand at the entrance and I actually feel goosebumps to know that those people are probably hearing everything we are saying.

"What's next?" I croak.

He closes the door and we move on to the room where he sits to code. There is nothing in that room, just white walls, a plain black table and a leather swivel chair.

I turn to him. "That's it?"

He nods. "That's it. When I am coding, I want no distractions at all. This room is sound proofed too. Even the smallest distraction could mean days or hours of work being undone. Here is where I sit in complete silence and travel backwards in my mind over the hundreds of complicated sequences of codes I've written and try to weed out and correct any tiny mistakes I might have made."

When we finish the tour we end up in the great big room. I curl up on the couch.

"Want some coffee?" he asks staring at my legs

I pull my legs onto the sofa. "Um... no. Come sit with me for a while."

He sits on the sofa next to me and slides his hand up my thigh. "Jesus, I can never get enough of you. Open your legs."

I spread my thighs and show him my pussy.

As his head moves to get between my thighs, I catch his face between my palms. "Konstantin?"

"Yeah."

"Konstantin?"

"Yeah."

"Is there anything in your office that you couldn't bear to be apart from?'

He looks at me as if I'm talking a foreign language. "My office?"

"Yes. Is there some furniture, some files, some paintings that are important to you?"

He doesn't have to think about it. "No."

"Then would you mind if I redecorated it?"

He stares at me, but his eyes are still hazy with lust. "You want to redecorate my office?"

"Yeah. I know this must sound like the craziest thing you've ever heard, but it's always been my dream to redecorate an office. I promise, I won't change it too much. Maybe I'll move the paintings around and maybe give the walls a lick of paint. Maybe cream instead of that stark white. I might even buy a plant or two."

He pulls my hands away from his cheeks. "Go ahead, decorate to your heart's content." Then his warm mouth is on my pussy. I close my eyes. Today I will keep him away from his office. And tomorrow afternoon I will take some time off and start the decorating process.

And then I stop thinking and concentrate on the delicious waves of pleasure coming from between my legs.

RAINE

Konstantin tells me he will not be at his home from lunchtime onwards so I can go ahead and redecorate. He seemed surprised that I was in such a hurry, but there was no suspicion in his eyes.

I did not go into his office because I did not want them to hear my voice, but I told the two guys who turned up to stack all the paintings and take them to the spare room. It only takes them three hours to give the place a coat of cream paint. Then they move all the furniture back and all the paintings except the one I switched. That one goes on the wall in the spare room and the painting that was in the spare room is brought into the office.

That evening, I bring Konstantin into the room. "Do you like it?"

He looks around, then turns to me sheepishly. "Sorry, I can't see any difference."

I laugh. The first real laugh since I went to meet Catherine at the café. Even thinking of her now makes goosebumps rise on my skin. The first thing I saw when I picked up my phone from the Faraday cage was her two-word text. She must have sent it as soon as I hung the painting up, which confirmed that it had a listening device hidden in it. *Good Job*

"I'm glad," I tell Konstantin. "I held back because I wanted to keep the change subtle."

"You seem happier, and more relaxed today," he observes.

"I am happier. I was a bit tense yesterday, but today I'm happy. Life is good."

"Hey, you know what I realized this morning after you had left for work?"

"What?"

"You didn't wear the sexy sex outfit you got in London last night."

I look at him from under my eyelashes. "I'm wearing it now... Sir."

He laughs. "Did you just call me Sir?"

"Yes, Sir."

"Oh, you are in so much trouble."

"What kind of trouble am I in, *Sir*? Is it bad enough for me to be punished?"

He doesn't answer me. He strips off my clothes until I am standing in the little pink baby doll nightie and suspenders and I hear him draw in his breath and make a small growling sound in his throat. It is animalistic and primal.

The jolt, from the sudden sexual pang I feel, is brutal. And just like that, the air between us becomes heavy and urgent. And our connection, charged and complex.

Wordlessly, I put my finger on his chest and push at him. He allows the light pressure to move him backwards until his thighs hit his desk. He rests his butt on the edge. As I get on my knees, his beautiful eyes go molten with lust.

I nudge his thighs apart till his legs are on either side of me. Then I hook my hand in the waistband of his pants and his briefs and pull them down his hips. He lifts his ass to assist me, and I pull the material the rest of the way down. I can't explain it, but seeing his cock so thoroughly exposed in an office setting arouses me, makes me wet with desire. The pale delicate skin, lined with bulging veins is throbbing with excitement. Like a child reaching for a new toy, I grab his erect cock. It jerks as I make contact, but as I wrap my hand around the thick, heavy shaft, I feel him swell even more.

My own sex pulses as I lower my head and stretch my mouth over the wide crest of his cock.

I hear his sharp intake of breath... and relish the response.

Hollowing my cheeks, I give the head a hard suck. A grunt of unbearable pleasure falls from his lips. I double down on my suction, my grip of him, hard. My hands fist him, moving up and down his hardness, in fluid, rhythmic strokes.

When I release my mouth from around him, a small burst of pre-cum swirls on my tongue and his jaw is clenched with the intense pleasure of my actions. I stick my tongue out and lap him up, but greedily, unashamed of my own hunger for him. The tip of my tongue twists around his head, then licks its way down the entire length of his shaft.

His fingers dig into my hair, and I move even lower to meet his balls, heavy with arousal, and take as much of them as I can in my mouth. My heart is fluttering, and I'm so turned on that molten desire drips from my sex and runs down the inside of my thighs.

"Goddamn it... Raine," he shudders, closing his eyes in ecstasy.

I fist him even harder, then prepare to take as much of him into my mouth as I can. Heated and wet, I sink down on him from the tip and slide all the way down to the middle of his length. That is as far as I can go without choking. The tip of his shaft is already brushing the back of my throat. I pull away, the slurping sounds, resounding across the room and mixing with the sound of his heavy breathing.

I tighten the muscles of my mouth even more and begin to milk him, my head bobbing up and down at a moderate pace.

He begins to writhe gently over me, his eyes shoot open to watch me. His eyes are wide with wonder, and sweat beads across his forehead. I love his completely unguarded, almost haunted look, enthralled at the fact that I'm beginning to unravel him just as he has done to me so many times.

Soon, my hand joins in the worship, gripping him, I viciously pump the wicked, wicked shaft. My rhythm increases as I feel his hips begin to instinctively thrust from the delicious agony. I see his hand grip the edge of the table so hard his knuckles turn white.

I can tell he is ready to climax, but I don't want him to come yet. I want to torment him a little longer. I withdraw my mouth. Tilting my head, I begin to place wet hot kisses up and down the shaft.

"Finish the job, Raine," he grates.

I take pity on him and milk him once again.

He responds with a guttural almost haunting groan, then suddenly comes with a roaring shout. Hot cum bursts from his cock, into my mouth, and flows down my throat. I swallow it and never stop sucking until his body stills, until there is no more to be milked. Licking my lips, after swallowing every bit of his release, I'm about to rise when I see his hands violently gripping the edge of the desk. I look up and see his face is strangely tense.

Hell, he's not finished.

His head is thrown back and his body jerks suddenly as he strokes the shaft himself, and keeps coming, the thick liquid spraying over my chest. I quickly grab the rogue cock and slip it back into my mouth to soothe it. I keep on sucking it until he is finished. Finally, he looks down on me.

I find his eyes misty and full of astonishment. This has never happened to him before. Instantly, my heart swells to bursting. At that moment, I'm so happy I almost want to float away, completely overcome with a wild and incomparable bliss.

I did that. I made his eyes fill with wonder and wild emotion.

Me, little, inexperienced, farm girl, Raine Fillander.

RAINE

We sit on the terrace sipping Mai Tai cocktails. The sun has already set and the stars are starting to show in the darkening sky. It is very beautiful and tranquil. I turn to Konstantin and find him watching me intently.

"What is it?" I ask softly.

"Today my assistant found someone else who is the right match to donate bone marrow to your sister."

My jaw drops with astonishment. "No. The cost of the procedure will sky rocket."

"The money is not important," he says quietly. "I don't want you to suffer."

I leave my chair and go to kneel next to him. I touch his face tenderly. Day by day my love for him grows deeper and deeper. Sometimes I am afraid I will become one of his desperate exes but I cannot help myself. He is so amazing.

"You don't understand. I want to do it for Maddy. It is my pleasure to suffer for her."

He leans his forehead against mine and sighs. "I don't like it, but as you wish."

"Thank you for everything you have done for us. I don't know if I will ever be able to repay you, but my mother wants to thank you herself. She wants to invite you over to dinner. Our home is very small and cramped, but do you think you could bear to accept her invitation if it is just for an hour or so?"

He puts his fingers over my mouth. "Why do you say things like that when you know I've been very poor for a long time? All this money is nice to have, but there are far more important things in life."

"Like the secret project you're working on?" I blurt out without meaning to.

He stills. "Yes."

"I know you can't tell me about it, so let's just change the subject."

"No, wait. I want to tell you. I trust you." He pulls me into his lap and I lean against his chest and look up into his face.

"What do you know about singularity?"

"Absolutely nothing," I confess.

"The definition of singularity is a hypothetical point in time when technological growth becomes uncontrollable and irreversible, resulting in unforeseeable changes to human civilization. Now, it may seem to the ordinary person that moment is far away in the future, but he would be very wrong to think that. Our civilization is actually moving at breakneck speed towards humanity+."

I gaze into his eyes. "Humanity+?"

"It's another way of describing transhumanism."

"Ah, the merging of humans with machines and the rise of the superhuman."

He strokes my hair. "That's the Hollywood movie version, and how transhumanist proponents sell the idea to the public. Humans accessing the internet without having to plug something into their bodies must mean the interface with the machines can better serve humans. But if you study the scientific papers they publish, you will quickly find that what they tell you is a barefaced lie. In fact, it is about giving the machine better access and control of the human body. It is about monitoring what goes on inside the human body: synthetic telepathy and reading our emotions. It goes without saying that if you can read it out, then you can also play it in using the same channel. Transhumanism it turns out is the perfect method of control. It is the wet dream of every government and every control crazed sociopath. They will be able to decide how you feel and what you think."

"Jesus!" I exclaim, shocked. "That's what transhumanism is truly about?"

"Yes. Without going into the complicated scientific explanations of encapsulated quantum dots, DNA absorbing light photons, and nanotubes and fibres, that is the simplest way I can explain it to you."

I lean away from him. "That sounds terrible. Why would anyone want to do that to themselves?"

"The problem is most people will not understand what they are getting into. They will not do their own research. They are too busy putting food on the table and paying their bills. They will simply Google it, and since Google is one of the major players in the push towards transhumanism, it is unlikely they find the truth anywhere on Google's search results. Once they have Googled it they will feel they have done their due diligence, Next step is to go ahead and sign up to become a superhuman. The effect will only become apparent when the machine has taken over, when it is too late."

I shake my head in wonder. "Would governments really do that to their own people? I mean, I can hardly believe it."

"Governments have poisoned and killed their own citizens since time immemorial. As I said before, the research and implementation is going at breakneck speed. They are almost at the cusp of rolling it out. All they need is an excuse which they will create at their pleasure. There is only a small window of opportunity left to warn people not to fall for the trick.

"Is that what you are doing, warning people?"

"No. That's not my expertise. I am building an alternative internet platform."

"An alternative internet? Why?"

"The time will come when anyone who is not part of the AI hive mind will be prohibited from utilizing the internet. That is when our system will come alive. It will be separate from their centralized internet and exist completely outside their control. Which means they can never shut it down."

At that moment I think of the painting. "There are people trying to stop you, aren't there?"

"Yes, there are very powerful people trying very hard to stop us, but our alliance is very strong and we have a secret advantage they do not know about."

I can't stop thinking about the painting. It bothers me that Catherine has never contacted me since I moved it to the spare room. What if it's not a listening device? What if it's something else I don't understand? I decide to get rid of the painting tomorrow.

"I'm leaving for Amalfi, in Italy tomorrow night. I'm going there to meet a Russian hacker. I'll be staying there for two days in a small, old fashioned hotel built into a cliff. It won't be glamorous, but will you come with me?"

I chew my bottom lip. "I'd love to, Konstantin, but I have to work."

"You were working two jobs to pay for your sister's medical bills. You don't have them anymore, why not give one up?"

"You're right. I don't know why I'm still doing it. Maybe it's just a habit."

"Give your notice and come with me."

"All right."

BLAKE LAW BARRINGTON

"What good fortune it is for governments that people do not think."
-Adolf Hitler

I put the phone down after speaking to Konstantin and swivel my chair around to stare out of the window. Things are starting to happen, but I can't help feeling worried. There is a tight ball of anxiety in my gut. It is all too easy. I alone, from everyone in our group, understands our enemy. I know because I am their spawn.

Only I know how utterly ruthless and powerful they are.

The others are full of hope, zeal, and innocence. They have never met the enemy. Only I have seen their faces and known their dastardly deeds. Only I know how depraved they are. It is almost impossible to tell the others about them. They will wither away in shock. The human mind cannot conceive of the pure evil that lurks in the true psychopath. He is actually insane. He looks totally normal, he functions perfectly, and can blend into society seamlessly, he may even be considered charming, but he is criminally and irreparably insane.

And it is his kind that rules our world.

There is a quick knock on my door and my oldest son, Sorab, comes into the room. I swivel around and smile at him. Every time I see him my heart swells with pride. He is seven now, and it is almost impossible for me to think of him as humanity's hope, but if I do this right, he will be. One day, he will battle the dark forces that seek to destroy life as we know it and win.

"Hi, Dad," he says, as he uses his palms to hoist himself onto my desk next to me.

"Hi," I reply. Just by looking at his face I can tell something is troubling him.

"Dad?"

"Yeah?"

"Why can't I have a smartphone? *All* the other kids do," he complains.

"Because smartphones are bad for kids."

"But if smartphones are so bad how come all the other parents allow their kids to have them?"

"What does it matter what other people do?" I ask gently. "If something is wrong, it is wrong, and *you* shouldn't do it."

"I don't understand what is so wrong about it. I just want to play some games, talk to my friends."

"Tomorrow when you go to school, I want you to watch your friends while they are on the phone. I want you to watch their faces. You see them staring at their screen with a vacant expression in their faces. Do you know why that is?"

He stares at me, his eyes as blue as mine. Only they have not seen the horrors I have.

"No," he replies sulkily.

"Because they are in a literal state of hypnosis as they automatically and mindlessly browse and scroll while losing track of time and the world around them. Each additional daily hour of screen time increases the child's risk of becoming addicted, or even affecting his or her long term mental health."

"But, Dad. I only want to use it for short periods. I promise I won't use it for ages and ages like the other kids. I don't want to be the only one who doesn't have one."

"Okay. So you'll only use it for a short time. During that short time you are in a state of hypnosis, who and what is going to have a direct line into your head?"

"What do you mean?"

"Do you think what you have on the net comes out of nowhere? It is produced by corporations that are only interested in profit. They do not care for you. In fact, they want you to become addicted so you will keep on browsing mindlessly for the rest of your life."

"Don't the other parents know that?" he asks.

I shrug. "Some do and don't care because they want a bit of peace, others have no idea they are not only giving amoral corporations direct access to their children, but also allowing them to shape their young minds into whatever they want."

"Yeah, but I'm the only one who doesn't have one," he mutters, looking gloomily at his feet.

"I know it's hard for you, but you know, you're not like all the other kids, right? You have to be ready for when they come for you."

He lifts his head and looks at me. I feel my heart break at the expression on his face. He just wants to be a kid, but he can't because we are one of the hidden thirteen bloodlines of intergenerational wealth families the conspiracy theorists talk about. For hundreds of years we have ruled from the shadows until I stepped out. Said no. They still want my son. They will come for him and he must be ready to stand up to them or they will destroy him.

"Yeah, I know," my son says sadly.

"Good. I love you, my dear, dear son and I will give up my life to protect you. Always remember that."

He smiles. "Smartphones are stupid anyway."

I ruffle his silky hair. He gets that from his mother. "That's my boy. Shall we go practice some Jiu Jitsu?"

He jumps off the desk eagerly. "Okay, Dad."

RAINE

https://www.youtube.com/watch?v=b_zHQ6kFuQo
The Power Of Love

We travel during the night and arrive in Amalfi in the afternoon. The sky is azure and the sun is a white in the sky, and I can taste the salt of the ocean in the air. I instantly fall in love with the town with its cobblestone streets and its colorful houses. It is picture postcard pretty.

Our hotel is small and cute. It is also very old fashioned. Once you step through the wooden doors into the cool air inside, it is like you have gone back in time. Or stepped into the movie set of Casablanca. We walk to the reception where a portly man in a waistcoat checks us in by writing our names with a fountain pen into a narrow book. Then he hands over a large metal key with a yellowing paper tag on which the room number is written in ink.

Talk about old-fashioned.

The bellhop, a chatty boy in his teens, shows us to our room. As Konstantin tips him, I walk over to the window. To my surprise, I realize the hotel is actually at the edge of a cliff. There is a sheer drop below to the sea. The ocean sparkles in the sunlight.

I hear the door close and turn around. "Why this hotel?"

"Because the walls are so thick no one can hear you scream," he teases.

I grin. "And the other reason?"

"There is no internet or surveillance cameras."

"Ah, right."

"Do you feel like having Italian ice cream?"

"What kind of question is that? Of course, I do."

He smiles at me. "Let's go."

So we go out for a walk in the town. It is colorful with tourists. Konstantin takes me to a *Gelateria* and treats me to the most delicious ice cream I have ever tasted in my life. We sit on a wooden bench facing the sea and eat it. Very soon there are big seagulls flying around us. Their wing spans are quite impressive. Their eyes are beady and somehow give the impression of cold creatures, but they are so tame they land on the ground close to us.

They want to share our food. I break off bits of my cone and throw the pieces to them. They fight over the scraps and Konstantin breaks off his cone and throws it to them. The gesture shows me the heart of the man. Generous. He is generous.

And I think how very, very lucky I am.

We go into a quaint old shop where I buy a big box of sweets, pastries, a bottle of good olive oil, artichokes, and local cheeses for my mom and Maddy. Everything looks so fresh and real, even some of the fruit and vegetables being sold are misshapen as if they came off a small family owned farm.

We go back to the room and while I am in the bath Konstantin goes to meet the hacker who is also staying in one of the hotel's rooms. He is back while I am still in the bath so he comes into the bathroom and gently washes me.

We end up on the old-fashioned bed, which creaks. We laugh until we can laugh no more. We go to dinner in a seafood restaurant. Always when I am with Konstantin I have the impression I am in a dream. One day I will wake up and it will all be gone. It is what I feel when the waiters come to our table. They are all outrageous flirts and flatters.

They strip you with their hot eyes, but they do it all with such flamboyant flair you cannot take offence. It is all part of the dining experience. When we get back to the room, Konstantin falls on me. Apparently, he did take offence. He is wild with lust. Like an animal he claims me as his and... only his.

Again and again. All night long.

I go to sleep with the sound of the sea crashing on the rocks below. I am in a dream. A beautiful dream. When I wake up the sun is high in the sky. I turn and watch Konstantin, but he is already awake and watching me.

"Hey," he whispers.

"Have you been watching me sleep?"

"Is that creepy?"

"It would be if it was not you," I whisper. I nearly blurt out then that I have fallen in love with him, but I hold myself back. There will be time later. No need to rush. No need to rush at all.

"You look like an angel when you sleep. All that blonde hair is like a halo, and your skin is so flawless... you're so beautiful."

"My mouth is too big for me to be considered beautiful," I mumble, slightly embarrassed by his compliments.

"Your mouth is perfect. My cock fits perfectly in it."

"Ugh... the things you say," I complain, pulling my pillow out from under my head and try to smack his head with it, but he catches it and rolls on top of me, his hard shaft pressing against my thigh.

"I love your mouth," he growls possessively. "Every time I see it I want to either fuck it or fuck you."

I stare into his eyes. In the sunlight pouring in from the windows they look so beautiful. "So what's stopping you now?" I challenge.

"Sometimes I can hardly believe you're real," he murmurs almost to himself. "Can someone so innocent and pure really exist in this day and age?"

Instantly, I remember the painting. I am not pure and innocent. Until I tell him about it, what we have is a lie. The thought is painful. It ruins the dream. To forget I push him off me. He allows me to. Then I shimmy down and take his cock in my mouth.

The whole time he watches greedily as his big erect cock disappears between my lips and goes into my throat.

KONSTANTIN

https://www.youtube.com/watch?v=DeumyOzKqgI

The call from Thorne comes as soon as we touch down in the US.

"Meet me at the usual," he says, and the line goes dead.

I know instantly that something has gone very wrong.

I toss my phone into my briefcase and put it on top of my suitcase in the car. Then I ask my chauffeur to drive Raine back to her apartment.

"Where are you going?" she asks, a frown on her forehead.

"Remember, the less you know the better," I say, before I kiss her goodbye.

Then I hail a cab. As the cab makes it way slowly through the city traffic, I stare impatiently out of the window. For Thorne

Blackborne to call me directly on my phone means something big has gone down and whatever it is concerns me.

When I get to the seedy little café designated as our meeting place, I nod at the man at the register, and go straight to the back of it. I run up the threadbare carpet on the stairs and knock at one of the two doors on the first floor.

"Come," Thorne calls.

As I open the door I see him rising from one of the armchairs and come towards me. He looks troubled.

"What's wrong?"

"Vasilly is dead."

"What?" I explode.

"He was murdered last night."

I blink with shock. "How?"

"Stabbed in his room."

"Stabbed in his room?" I echo blankly. In my mind I can still see him, nervous, but determined to do his best. He offered me Vodka that he had brought from Russia. We sat together for five minutes drinking and talking. A good man. And young. So young. He has a family too. A wife and a little girl. Then we shook hands and I left.

"They're coming for you," Thorne says.

I nod. I already understood that.

"Who did you tell?"

I can't think. I don't want to think. "Tell?"

Thorne scowls. "Who knew you were meeting him?"

"No one." I swallow hard. "Only the girl. Only Raine."

A shadow passes his eyes. "Then it is her."

I shake my head. "No. It is not her."

"I'm sorry, Konstantin," he says softly. "I will start to make preparations. Do what you have to." Then he goes to the door and opens it. I stand in the middle of the room and listen to his footsteps die away. My hands clench into fists. There must be another explanation. There must be. And yet, I know, just as Thorne did, that there is no other explanation.

My first instinct was right.

She was always the honey trap. Always.

I just made the mistake of thinking with my dick.

RAINE

https://www.youtube.com/watch?v=vGwIaLojOUg
Think Twice

We're still sitting at the kitchen table eating the sweets and delicacies I brought back from Amalfi and talking about all the things I had seen when my phone pings with a text from Konstantin.

I'm on my way to your apartment.
Call me when you get outside.

I spring out of my chair instinctively.

"What's going on?" my mom asks.

"He's coming here and he wants me to go outside and meet him."

"He, as in Konstantin?" Maddy asks eagerly.

I nod blankly.

"Well, ask him to come up then," Mom says.

"Yes, ask him to come up. I want to thank him myself."

I nod, but distractedly. My antenna is up. Something is not right. I knew something was not right from the moment he got that phone call as we disembarked from the plane. I leave the apartment and run down the corridor. I call the elevator and can barely stand still while I wait for it to arrive. When it comes, I rush inside and jam my hand on the button with the faded G printed on it.

I stare impatiently at the lighted floors as the old elevator slowly makes its way down. As soon as I get outside I call him. To my surprise, he is standing about ten feet away, watching me. I run up to him. His eyes are so cold and distant I come to a dead stop a few feet away from him.

"What's wrong?"

"Let's walk," he says.

We walk in silence until we get to a small playground. He turns towards me.

"Vasilly is dead."

My jaw drops with shock. "The Russian hacker?"

There is absolutely no emotion in his face. "Yes."

"How?"

"Murdered last night in his room."

"How can that be? You met him last..." Suddenly it dawns on me. "He was murdered after you left him."

"No one else knew about my trip, about my meeting, except you."

I take a step back in shock. "What? You don't think I had anything to do with it. How could—" I stop suddenly. I can feel the blood draining from my face.

"Who did you tell?" he asks, taking a step forward. I can see hope in his face. He thinks I'm going to give him a name. He thinks I'm innocent. He wants me to be innocent.

I can no longer hide what I have done. "I didn't tell anyone about the trip I swear, but I'm not innocent."

The light in his eyes dies. They stare at me listlessly. "Tell me what happened."

I freeze. This was not the way I intended to tell Konstantin of my secret, but here this was it. The moment of truth was here.

"I wasn't at the auction by chance. I was paid $50,000 by a woman on behalf of her client to be there. All of the girls you saw that night were paid by her. We were paid to be there and if we were picked by you we had to switch one of the paintings in your office. I was told that the painting had sentimental value to someone important and you had stolen it and he wanted it back. I know it sounds like complete nonsense to you, and it does to me too now, but at that time I was desperate for money. I would have done almost anything to get the money to save Maddy and it seemed like such an innocent simple thing to do. What harm could it do? You have to understand, Konstantin, I didn't know anything about your secret project or the kind of man you were. I just thought you were another selfish billionaire. I was stupid."

"So you switched the painting?" he asks icily.

"Yes, I switched it. I had no choice. I understood by the time we came back from London that I had been completely duped. I tried to give them the money back and refused to do the job, but when I told them they threatened to hurt Maddy and Mom if I did not complete the deal. I guessed the painting was most probably a listening device, so I devised a plan to do the job without actually doing it. I hung the picture up and I took it away the very next day by pretending to redecorate your office. I thought that I had solved the problem by putting it away in one of your spare rooms, but apparently, I hadn't."

Something flashes in his eyes, but it is gone as quickly as it had come. "Is it still in the spare room?"

"No, I didn't even trust it to be there so I threw it away."

"But it was too late. I made my travel arrangements known to them that morning before you got into decorate the room."

I reach out a hand towards him. "I'm sorry, I'm so, so, so sorry, Konstantin."

He takes a step back from me. "You betrayed me. You had so many chances to tell me and you didn't."

I just stand there staring at him, pleading with my eyes, but he doesn't soften. He looks at me with disgust. He doesn't understand. I had no choice. They were going to hurt innocent little Maddy. I did my best in the circumstances.

"I never want to see you again," he says, his voice hard. It hits me like a bullet to my heart.

I actually sway with horror. "I never knew what was at stake. I didn't know my actions would get a man murdered."

For a split second I see something in his eyes. A torment. A terrible sadness. I see him swallow hard. "You didn't get him murdered. He was a dead man walking. All you did was help them set the bear trap I walked into."

"How?"

"They are trying to frame me for his murder."

"But you didn't do it. I will testify that you were with me the whole night."

He shakes his head. "No, you won't."

"Yes, I will," I cry desperately.

"You have no idea what you have got yourself into."

"What are you talking about?"

"There will be no more money for Maddy's treatment so you will sell yourself to the highest bidder again."

I stare at him aghast. "You're not going to pay for Maddy anymore?"

"Should I?"

I stare at him in disbelief. Everything, everything has been shattered into a million pieces.

He takes one last look at me, then he grits his teeth and walks away. I watch him, his long legs striding further and further away from me.

The dream is over.

The nightmare has begun. For Konstantin. For me. For Mom. And for poor, little Maddy.

RAINE

Mom calls me to ask where I am. I'm too choked to talk about it so I tell her I'm running an errand and I'll be back home soon. I walk to a bench and sit down. There is a little girl in a pair of brown dungarees. She pushes herself higher on the swing than any of the other children. I watch her mindlessly.

How happy and carefree she seems to be.

I can't remember the last time I was like that. Maybe when we were still living on the farm. Her mother calls to her and she doesn't wait for the swing to come to a stop before she flies off it. I watch as they walk away from the playground. Then I stand and start to walk home.

Maddy is in the bath and my mom is getting ready to go to work. I want to tell her that Maddy's operation has been cancelled but I just can't bring myself to do it. I sit at the kitchen table and try to think. I just need to think. There must be a way out of this.

When Mom comes into the kitchen I make some excuse to explain away why Konstantin didn't come up.

"Ah, well. Never mind. We'll get to meet him when he comes here for dinner."

"Yes," I say softly.

"Right. I better be off. Will you be spending the night here or at his place?"

"Er... here I guess."

"All right then. See you later. Take the chicken out of the freezer in about three hours, won't you?"

"Yes, Mom."

As soon as she leaves, I rush to my room and lie on my bed. The last thing I want to do is talk to Maddy. I feel so guilty I can't even look at her hope-filled face. She never looked like that until I told her that her treatment was all covered and going through. That she was going to be fine again. And now I'm about to pull the rug out from under her.

I throw myself on my bed and switch on the small TV in my room so she will not come in. I stare at the screen without really taking any of it in. All I am thinking of is how I can undo what I have done, to Konstantin, to Mom, and to Maddy. I want to cry, but I won't let myself.

Until a piece of news catches my attention and pulls me out of my misery. I sit up and immediately increase the volume.

It is a breaking story about the mysterious stabbing of a Russian man believed to be a computer hacker in a hotel room in Italy. A Russian billionaire living in the States is being questioned in connection with this death, but they are not releasing more details at the present moment.

The newscaster moves on to the next story and I slump back on the bed. Suddenly, my phone rings. I jump to it. It is an unknown number. I click accept.

"Hello," I say cautiously.

"Hello, my dear. This is Helena Barrington. We met at the Iserby's party."

I feel a cold, cold hand clutch at my belly.

"I was wondering if you'd like to have some tea with me. My driver will pick you up in about an hour."

I'm too surprised to even answer her, but she carries on as if I have agreed.

"Good. I'll see you when you get here."

Then the line goes dead. I stare at my phone. Then I jump up and begin to pace my bedroom floor. How did she get my number and what does she want with me? I remember Konstantin telling me that I will not help him and that I had no idea what I had got myself into. Is this what he meant? Was she going to ask for my help?

I consider calling her and telling her I won't be coming, but something stops me. Not going will not help me or anyone else. I should go to meet the woman I am sure is the enemy so that I know what she is planning. Perhaps she will reveal something that I could use to help Konstantin.

First I take the chicken out the freezer then I get into the shower. It feels wonderful to let the water pour down my head and body. As I stand under the warm cascade, my mind starts to clear. I'm determined to do everything in my power to undo the damage I have caused.

By the time I get out of the shower I am no longer tense and jittery. Instead, I feel unusually calm and collected. She won't beat me. I won't underestimate her, but I won't let her trick me. For sure, this is a trick. Konstantin thinks I betrayed him, that I can be bought and I will be bought by her, but I won't.

I'm smart, and I've always been good at finding solutions.

As I pass the living room, Maddy is staring at her cell phone and smiling. The blue light of the screen makes her appear almost unreal. The sight makes me frown. It reminds me of the way Konstantin had spoken of the AI and the way it would take over the human consciousness.

As soon as she gets better I will make sure that she goes out and has a life instead of living through her digital avatar.

Going to my room, I quickly dry my hair so it falls in a straight shiny curtain down my back which I then put into a ponytail on my head. Then I change into one of the beautiful silk blouses Jane had chosen for me in London. I team it with a gorgeous Hermes scarf and a burnt orange skirt. Then I step into an expensive pair of court shoes with thick classy heels, the kind that she would appreciate.

My phone pings. I look at it.

I am your driver and I am waiting outside for you.

I put my cell phone and credit cards into my brand-new designer purse and go into the living room. Maddy looks up from her screen. Her eyes widen.

"Wow! You look fabulous. Are you off to see the billionaire?" she teases.

"No, I'm off to see one of Konstantin's friends. I'll be back in time to make the dinner."

"Okay. Have fun."

"Thanks." Then I go downstairs to meet my fate.

RAINE

With artificial intelligence we are summoning the demon.
You know all those stories where there's the guy with the
pentagram and the holy water and he's like... yeah he's sure he
can control the demon... doesn't work out.
—Elon Musk

Helena Barrington's home is in Manhattan, facing
the southern end of Central Park. From what I
can see as I am led to meet her by a man with
large sad eyes, it appears to be set on at least four floors. In
terms of décor it is the opposite of what Konstantin's apartment looks like. Konstantin's apartment is modern and
minimal and hers is like a French palace. There are antiques,
statues, and old paintings, masterpieces I would guess,
hanging on the walls.

I am shown to a room with more Marie Antoinette style
furniture. The ceilings are tall and the room is at once grand
and intimidating. She is sitting on a cream sofa with a white
dog on her lap. She appears to me to be impervious, inflexi-

ble, and utterly cold. It is almost like looking into the eyes of a reptile. There is nothing there. No emotion at all. No warmth at all.

"Miss Raine Fillander," the manservant announces in a formal tone.

"Thank you, Horton. We are ready for tea whenever you are."

"Very good, Madam," he says, and withdraws, closing the door.

Her eyes scan me, noting all the designer stuff I have piled on myself. I can tell by the expression in her eyes that she has come to the impression I wanted her to get. She thinks I dressed this way because wearing expensive designer clothes is important to me.

"Come in and sit down," she invites.

I walk over and take the seat opposite her. "You have a very beautiful home."

"Thank you," she says, sounding bored.

Then her dog suddenly jumps off her lap and comes towards me.

"Cesar," she calls, but it ignores her and sniffs at my ankle.

"He's getting on now and if you sit still, he'll pee on your leg," she warns.

I don't look up at her. I know exactly what she is doing. I grew up on a farm. I know and understand animals better than I do humans. This dog is not going to pee on me.

A) There is no way this dog is not toilet trained.

B) There is no way anyone in their right mind is going to let a dog soil such a fine and expensive carpet.

She just wants to startle me, to put me at a disadvantage. Well, round one to me. I reach out a hand and scratch the top of its head and instantly, it stands on its hind legs and begs to come up on my lap. I pick it up and put it on my lap and look up at her. Just in time to see her eyes flash with fury. She is quick to veil it.

So... she is jealous of her dog liking anyone else.

But I don't want her to be angry and jealous. I don't want her to see me as a formidable opponent. I want her to underestimate me. Sun Tzu's advice reverberates in my head, *when able to attack, we must seem unable; when using our forces, we must seem inactive; when we are near, we must make the enemy believe we are far away; when far away, we must make him believe we are near.*

"I love all animals," I tell her. "I grew up on a farm, you see. You can take the girl from the farm, but you can't take the farm from the girl."

I put the dog back down on the carpet, and it wanders back to her. She pats her thighs and it jumps back onto her lap.

There is a soft tap on the door, before it opens and three women of either Mexican or South American descent appear. They are wearing black and white maids' uniforms and wheeling trolleys of food. As I stare in surprise the women load all the food onto the table. There are all kinds of sandwiches, bagels, cakes, pastries, doughnuts, and pots of tea.

I look up at her and find her watching me speculatively. "I didn't know what you liked," she murmurs.

"That was kind of you," I say politely, but I feel the first real sense of unease. Is this woman even sane?

One of the maids pours tea into the gold-rimmed china cup in front of me.

"One sugar, thank you," I instruct with a smile.

Then the women leave and I am left alone with the reptilian like human.

"Please, eat," she urges.

The last thing in the world I want to do is eat, but I reach for a biscuit and nibble on it. "What did you want to see me about?"

"I heard that Konstantin has done what he does to all the women in his life. He casts them away when he is done with them. I understand he has also reneged on his promise to pay your sister's medical bills."

I don't pretend to ask how she knows. I know exactly how she knows and she knows I know. I put the biscuit down on the saucer of my cup as if I am too emotional to eat.

"Yes. Yes, he has," I say, making my voice sound choked and hoarse.

Her eyes glitter. "I'd like to help you."

I pretend to look surprised. "You do?"

She smiles. "Yes. How would you like to easily earn a million dollars?"

"A million. How?"

"The police will come to interview you about the death of that Russian hacker. All you have to tell them is you were asleep. You were so deeply asleep you couldn't be sure if Konstantin remained all night with you. He might have been, but he could just as easily not have been."

"But won't that mean he could end up in prison?"

"Not necessarily. It will be up to his defense team to come up with an appropriate defense. You just won't be supplying him with an alibi." She leans forward. "He doesn't deserve it. He promised to pay for your sister's medical bills and now even though she has nothing to do with the mess he finds himself in, he is punishing her. I think that is despicable behavior."

I nod slowly. "Yes, it is despicable behavior. I suppose I won't really be telling a lie. I do sleep soundly and there could have been many instances during the night when he could have left to murder that poor man and got back into bed with me."

I pause, as if I am considering my options. She says nothing.

"Um... when will I get the money?"

"As soon as you have testified at the trial."

I widen my eyes. "I have to testify in court?"

"Of course."

"Does that mean I will be cross examined?"

"Yes, but if you stick to your heavy sleeper story, there is not a thing they can do."

"Won't going to court take a very long time?"

"I am reliably informed Konstantin's case will be expedited by the judge. He will stand trial in less than two months."

I frown. "But my sister needs her treatment before that."

"I have spoken to a specialist in the matter, your sister can easily survive for the next six months."

"Okay. I'll do it for Maddy."

"Wonderful." Her voice is full of triumph.

She thinks she's got me.

RAINE

"We are probably one of the last generation of homosapians. Within a century or two, earth will be dominated by entities that are more different from us than we are different from Neanderthals, or from chimpanzees. Because in the coming generations, we will learn how to engineer bodies, and brains, and minds."

– Yuval Noah Harari,
World Economic Forum,

When I get home I cook the chicken and Maddy and I eat together. As I watch her eat, I hope and pray I have made the right decision for her. It may all go wrong, but this is the right thing to do.

For the first time I'm doing what is right.

Maddy shows me a TikTok video she has found online. I smile at it. She takes the phone from me and starts scrolling through it and for a second, I feel strange fear grip me. The way she is staring at the screen, lost inside that world, makes me think of Konstantin's words. They want us to be connected to the machine. My sister will be one of those people who will think it is a great idea to take something that will internally connect her. She will never have to worry about reception or her battery running out.

She has a terrible paranoia about that.

After we have eaten and the dishes have been washed, we sit in front of the TV in the living room watching Stranger Things. I find it impossible to concentrate. I keep thinking of Helena Barrington. I remember the way Lana almost shrank with fear when Konstantin told her husband she had a message for him. I must not underestimate Helena. She is not just a formidable opponent, but a fearful, ruthless, infinitely powerful one.

If she can strike fear in the hearts of her own son and daughter-in-law I have to tread very, very carefully. Eventually, the episode ends and Maddy goes off to bed. I sit staring at the TV until my mother comes in. She looks haggard today.

"Are you all right, Mom?"

"Yeah. It'll be good when I can stop this job at the end of the month."

I swallow. I gave them all hope and now I'm about to take it all away. I walk up to her and put my finger against my lips. I take her cell phone from her pocket and put it on the side table. She says nothing as I lead her towards the front door. We say nothing while we stand in the lift. She stares at me as if her heart is breaking. She already knows I have bad news for her.

We get to the street and start walking.

"What's going on, Raine?" she asks.

I tell her everything. About Konstantin's secret alliance and what they are doing, about the murder of the hacker, about him finding out my betrayal, his reneging on his offer to pay my sister's medical bills, about Helena Barrington's one million dollars. Her face becomes white as a ghost and her eyes are filled with horror.

Then I tell her my plan.

She clasps her hands together tightly. "Are you sure, Raine?"

I nod. "I have never been more sure of anything in my life."

"But she sounds so dangerous... so evil."

"Yes, she is very dangerous and evil, but this is the right thing to do. No matter what happens after, this is the right thing to do."

"What if she arranges to hurt or even kill you?"

"There are worse things than death, Mom. We are all going to become slaves, controlled by a central AI, if Helena's side wins. I make this sacrifice willingly."

"And Maddy?"

"I think I know how to get help for Maddy too. Let me work on it then I'll tell you all about it."

We say nothing until we get back to the apartment. When we get in, I turn to her. "Are you hungry, Mom?"

"No."

"Shall we just have some chocolate ice cream?"

"Yes, lets."

We sit together at the kitchen table and eat our ice cream. This is the calm before the storm. Soon the police will come to interview me and the whole merry-go-round will start. They will arrest him. They will charge him with murder. Their plan is to break the alliance. I remember the story of the poor little Dutch boy who put his finger in a hole in the dike to stop the water from rushing through and bursting open the old dike, and drowning his entire country. I am that little boy. It is only my finger in the leaking dike that stands between the alliance winning and the end of humanity as we know it.

Suddenly, my mother's hand shoots out and grasps mine. "I'm proud of you, Raine. Very proud."

I smile at her. I don't let her see my heart is shattered. The man I love is lost forever.

RAINE

https://www.youtube.com/watch?v=eM213aMKTHg&
ab_channel=LadyAVEVO
Need You Now

Three weeks pass. I go through the days in a daze. The police call me to come to the station and take my statement, and I find out that Konstantin is out on a five million bail.

At first I keep looking at my phone, thinking, hoping Konstantin will call, but he never does. By the middle of the second week I know he is never going to call.

There is another change in me. I have started to view my phone with extreme suspicion. Now that I understand it is recording my conversations and locations I treat it as a necessary evil. In fact, I am even thinking of getting an analogue phone. That way I can communicate with people, but my conversations won't be recorded and used for nefarious purposes. I go to Lois's home and see that she has an Alexa, and my first instinct is to immediately suggest we leave.

But it is when I see how utterly entranced my sister is with her phone, that I feel real pain. I actually feel the same way someone must if they see their loved ones shooting heroin into their veins.

I know I must bide my time. Be patient. She is ill and other than the small walk she is allowed every day to give her some fresh air and keep her muscles exercised, she has nothing to look forward to in her life.

Once she is better I will wean her away from that device and back to the real world.

Mom doesn't give her notice. She is unsure of our future and she wants to carry on working for the time being. I just nod even though it breaks my heart to see how tired she is.

"Maddy, isn't it time you were in bed?"

"Yeah, yeah, I'm going," she says, and uncurls herself from the sofa.

"Goodnight," I say, switching off the TV.

"Nite, nite," she calls as she disappears into the room where she and Mom sleep in. I lean back and close my eyes. I can hear our neighbors arguing. They have taken to arguing a lot these days. Mom won't be home for another two hours tonight. She was offered overtime work and she took it.

I hear the ping of my phone and I am curious who would be texting me at this time of the night as I go to my bedroom and look at it. It is an unknown number. I open the text and stare at it with my heart racing.

It is just an address and the words. Come now.

I don't even think it could be a prank or a hoax or even a dangerous plot that could get me raped or murdered. Intuition tells me exactly who it is. I knock on Maddy's door and tell her I'm going out for a bit. As I make my way to the elevator, I send a message to my mom to say I might not be home when she comes in. I run into the street and hail a cab. I give the driver the address and sit back.

My stomach is in knots with sheer excitement. The address is not in the best part of town, in fact it is only a few blocks away. Under normal circumstances I would have walked. I pay the driver and run to the door. On the shiny surface of the elevator I see that my hair is a mess. I was in such a state I didn't even brush it before I left the house.

I comb my fingers through my hair quickly.

My eyes look feverish. I walk down the narrow corridor. I can hear the sounds of TV sets coming from the apartments on either side of me. I take a deep breath, knock on door number 632 and wait. The door opens, before I can say anything, Konstantin puts a finger on my lips.

He pulls me in and closes the door. For a few seconds, he does nothing, just looks at me, his eyes roving greedily over my face and body, then he catches me and whirls me around so my palms slam into the door.

He reaches in my skirt and tears away my panties. A small moan escapes my mouth, but he comes close to my ear and says, "Shhh..."

Then he tilts my hips upwards, crouches down, and swipes his velvety tongue slowly and tantalizingly along the crack of my sex. My stomach curls, but he doesn't stay for long. It is as if he just wanted one taste.

He stands and pulls me towards him. I press my body invitingly against his hardness. With the solid heat of his body pressed against me I feel strangely safe. As if the outside world with all its problems and horrors does not exist.

I feel him grab my hips roughly, and suddenly, without warning and without using any protection he enters me in a fierce thrust. My mouth opens in a startled gasp. He is branding me. It is crude, it is primitive, but it is exactly what I want. I need to take him raw. And if he leaves his seed in me even better.

He plunges in again, harder.

I gasp softly.

I feel him pull apart my buttocks and the next thrust is so hard and so deep that my body jerks like a puppet. My eyes swivel upwards, dimly noticing the ceiling that needs a new coat of paint. All that I need is to be his. Like this. Forever.

His skin slaps against mine as he fucks me so hard I feel his thighs chafe against mine. He comes inside me in a rush of heat. And I am glad for his seed. I wish one of them will grow inside me. If that is the only thing I can have from him, then so be it.

"Shhh..." he says again.

I become still.

He crouches down again and pushes my skirt up, and looks at my pussy. I can feel his seed leaking out of me. He puts a restraining hand on the small of my back, he licks my swollen sex. Then he does something strange. He opens the curls of my sex and whispers something right into my pussy. Then he licks me clean. Just like a dog.

My hips start to move. I want him to fill me up again. I've been so empty without him.

While his thumb circles my clit, he pushes his fingers into me and finger fucks me.

Until I climax, my mouth opening in a silent scream. He doesn't allow me to turn around and look him in the eye. He pulls me towards him, opens the door, and gives me a slight shove. The door closes and I'm standing in the corridor.

The sounds of the TV's follow me all the way to the elevator.

He's just treated me like shit, but I love him. I love him so much it hurts.

RAINE

Weeks pass and as Helena Barrington predicted the date of Konstantin's trial is set within two months of the time I went to her apartment. I mark the start of it on my calendar and cross another day off before I go to bed.

Life drags on.

Our little family seems to be in a limbo. I pretend to be normal, but it's hard and often I find I am berating myself. If only I had trusted Konstantin and told him earlier about the painting. But I can't go back and change the past. I can only make the future better by doing the right thing.

All Maddy knows is there is a slight delay to her procedure. Of course, she knows something is wrong, that Konstantin and I are no longer together, but she doesn't ask about him, or refer to him as 'the billionaire' the way she used to all the time.

Once I find my mom crying in the bathroom. Instantly, I assume something is wrong with Maddy, but I find out she is crying because of me.

I stare at her in surprise. "Me? Why me?"

She drags me over to the mirror. "Look at you," she says. "Just look at the state of you."

In the mirror, I see a stranger's face. It's true, there are shadows under my eyes and my face looks gaunt and haunted. I've stopped taking care of myself. I hardly look in the mirror anymore because I can't bear to look into my own eyes. I still feel so guilty, and until Maddy has her procedure I will not stop feeling bad. I can't help feeling I ruined it all, for me and Konstantin and for her by being a fool.

I turn away from my reflection and look at her. "It's okay, it'll be over soon, Mom."

"I'm not talking about that. I'm talking about something else."

I frown.

"You're pregnant, aren't you?"

My eyes widen. "I... I... why do you think that?"

"When are you due your period?"

My periods are never regular, but only then do I realize I am late. By more than a week.

"Yes, I thought so." She looks at me sadly. "I'm so sorry, honey."

I grip her hand fiercely. "Don't be sorry, Mom. I want this baby. You don't know how much."

She looks into my determined, passionate face and nods. "All right. We'll manage together. Somehow."

"It'll be fine, Mom. I promise. It'll be fine."

"Wait here," she says and leaves the bathroom. She comes back with two pregnancy kits and gives them to me. My mother leaves and I do the test. While I wait for the results I remember again that day when he entered me in that apartment. Not a single word passed between us, and anyone else would have thought it was a quick, rough, ugly encounter, but there was so much need in both of us. It was as if we were starving for each other's touch.

To think we conceived a child in that strange encounter. I look down at the stick. There are two clear lines on it.

I move to the mirror and for the first time in many weeks I look at myself. I touch my stomach and tears of joy fill my eyes. No matter what happens now I can never again regret everything that happened. Because if not for those things this beautiful miracle wouldn't have happened.

I tell Lois about my pregnancy.

"Are you going to keep it?" she asks, surprised.

"Of course I am. I want this baby."

"But you're not with him anymore. Why do you want his baby?"

"Because I love him. I love him, Lois. More than you could ever know."

"So what are you going to do?"

I shrug. "I still have fifty thousand in my bank. I might try to buy a small farm somewhere in a faraway land. Somewhere cheap like South America. Grow some vegetables, rear some chickens for their eggs. I fancy the idea of living off the land."

"Don't leave New York, please, Raine," she pleads.

"I haven't made up my mind yet, Lois. It's just a pipe dream at the moment."

She chews her bottom lip. "Aren't you going to tell him about the baby?"

"Of course I will."

"What do you think he'll do?"

"I don't know. He's pretty mad with me right now, but I don't think he can be mad with his own son or daughter."

"You know what I think?"

"What?"

"I think he won't let you leave New York. I think he'll want to be part of the baby's life. I think you'll have to put your South American dream on ice for a very, very long time. At least until your kid is eighteen years old, anyway."

Then, finally, I get a reply to the letter I sent to Lana Barrington. It was not difficult to track down such a notable woman with so many charitable causes.

What she says gladdens my heart and fills me with hope for the future. I don't tell anybody about the letter or its contents. I just burn the letter and go about my business. At least now I know that no matter what happens to me, Maddy is safe. Her procedure can go on even without me.

A small sigh of relief escapes from my mouth. Lana Barrington has just taken care of that problem for me.

RAINE

https://www.youtube.com/watch?v=orL-w2QBiN8
The Lonely Shepherd

The trial begins. The channels and newspapers are full of it. A friend of Putin and a billionaire is savory gossip. Even I get some press. People still remember that I was the girl Konstantin Tsarnov paid a million dollars to have one dinner date with.

I don't go to the courtroom, but religiously and obsessively watch and read everything I can lay my hands on about it. The prosecution believe Konstantin has a very strong motive. They have testimony from the hacker's wife that he was working on something big and that he was going to meet a Russian billionaire and negotiate a price with him. Those files are now missing and have been completely erased from his computer so the prosecution have built their case around the idea that something must have gone wrong with the negotiations which caused Konstantin, in the heat of the moment, to murder him and steal the files.

But it seems to me the prosecution doesn't have anything other than circumstantial evidence.

They have the vodka glass with Konstantin's fingerprints. They also have his fingerprints on the knife that was used to stab him, but Konstantin's lawyer says that Konstantin used that knife to slice a lemon to put into the still water they drank together. There are no surveillance tapes of the corridors in the hotel, but they have a video of the entrance of the hotel which shows no one entered the hotel that night that was not accounted for.

His lawyer tried to demolish that argument by saying the killer could have entered through the kitchen, but the prosecution was ready. They flew the owner of the hotel into America. He testified that no one can enter through the back entrance, because the kitchen is locked after seven pm and there is always kitchen staff hanging around the back.

I have to admit his testimony is very solid and it doesn't sound good for Konstantin. Slowly, I begin to realize a lot now rests on my testimony. I was Konstantin's alibi. If I could not vouch for him being in the room with me during the murder, I would basically be throwing him to the wolves.

In two days it will be my turn to testify.

Today I'm working a shift running the bar for Lois's manager. It is a black and white tie event at a hotel. It is only when I arrive that I realize it is a Russian function. Immediately, my stomach contracts with tension. It appears all the great and good of Russian society will be here. At first I think he is not going to make an appearance. Maybe he is keeping a low profile until the trial is over. I know how he guards his privacy and I am sure that will be even more true now.

Then I realize with shock that the event is being held for him. The entire elite Russian community worldwide have come together to show solidarity at what they see as a political and Anti-Putin concocted trial. Guests are flying in from all over.

Now my heart is racing in my chest and I can barely stand still. A man comes over and sits on one of the stools.

I smile at him. "What can I get you?"

"Why don't you surprise me?" he says, with a slow smile.

My smile dies a little. "How about Russian vodka?"

His smile widens. "Ah, beautiful and smart."

I move away. "One Russian vodka coming up."

I put the drink in front of him. "Hey, you're not busy yet, why don't you talk to me for a bit?"

I take a step back. "Yeah, sure."

"So you live in New York, huh?"

"Yes, you?"

"I live in Monaco."

I nod. "Nice."

"Have you been?"

I shake my head.

"I have a yacht parked in the Riviera. Want to come spend a few days?"

I'm about to answer him, when I feel my hair stand on end. I turn my head and see Konstantin walking towards the bar. He is looking directly at me and his face is like thunder. I feel myself shrink. I know he is mad with me, but I never realized the extent of his fury. He stops at the bar and completely ignoring me he addresses the man.

"Yuri," he says tightly.

"Ah, the man of the night," Yuri says standing. "I was just talking to this very lovely barmaid."

Konstantin turns to me, and there is an expression in his eyes I cannot decipher. I stand rooted to the spot.

"Hello, Raine," he says softly.

"Ah, you know each other," Yuri says. "I suppose this is my cue to melt away."

"Yes, get lost," Konstantin says rudely, not taking his eyes off me.

My eyes widen.

He stares at me hungrily. At that moment I know that he still wants me, but he won't allow himself to be with me because of what I did to him.

"You look beautiful," he says, his voice husky with emotion, then he strides away, his body erect and tall, without looking back. Even though I look hard, I never see him again for the rest of the night.

I will see him in court, I suppose.

RAINE

https://www.youtube.com/watch?v=kJQP7kiw5Fk
The Gambler

"Do you swear to tell the truth and nothing but the truth?"

I place my hand on the bible, please God, forgive me, and say, "I do."

I can't help it. My eyes move to Konstantin. He's wearing a dark suit, his face is impassive, and his eyes are on me. My gaze slides away. I need to be calm. I have rehearsed this many times. I will pretend he is not even here.

First the attorney for the defense comes up to me. Mr. Justin Horrowitz stands, a greying tall man, shoots his cuffs, and comes forward.

"Can you tell the Court what your relationship to the defendant is, Miss Fillander?"

"I'm not in a relationship with the defendant anymore."

"But you were in one during the time this murder was committed, were you not?"

"Yes."

"And you were with him on the day of the murder?"

"Yes."

"Did you notice anything unusual about the defendant on that day? Was he nervous? Angry? Upset? Worried?"

"No."

"In the time you knew the defendant would you have ever thought he could actually stab a man to death with a knife?"

"Objection, your honor. The witness is not a psychologist capable of making a proper analysis of the defendant's likelihood to kill in the heat of the moment."

"Your honor, Miss Fillander is not here as a professional witness. I am allowed to establish her personal opinion of his character and state of mind that night."

"I'll allow it." The judge turns to me. "You may answer the question."

"No. I never believed him capable of such a thing, but then again I never think that about anybody," I say quietly.

His attorney tries not to show how disappointed he is with my answer. "Did the defendant seem unhappy or stressed that night?"

"No."

"What about in the morning?"

"No."

"So he did not behave like a man who had just brutally and in cold blood killed a man?"

The prosecutor shoots to her feet. "Objection, your honor. He's leading the witness *again*."

"Sustained. Stop leading the witness, Counsel," the judge cautions sternly.

Konstantin's attorney comes closer to me. So close I can see the open pores in his skin. "Can you confirm you spent the whole night together?"

I sneak a look at Konstantin. He is staring at me with an intense expression in his eyes. "Yes, I can confirm that we spent the whole night together."

"Thank you, Miss Fillander." He walks away from me.

"Your witness," he says to the prosecution's lawyer.

The prosecutor is a sly, peroxide blonde woman. Her perfectly coiffured hair stays like a hard helmet around her face, her eyes are sharp, and her smile is as friendly as a great white shark.

She flashes me one of those.

"Can you describe the evening of the murder, Miss Fillander?"

"We went out to dinner, then we came back to our hotel. Uh... we were intimate, and then we fell asleep." That is my first lie. I give the impression we had sex once, and then went to sleep. The truth is we had sex all night long until dawn was in the sky.

"And once you fell asleep did you wake up again?"

"No." Second lie. I almost never slept all night.

"Are you a heavy sleeper, Miss Fillander?"

"Yes, I am." Third lie. I'm not.

"Did you wake up at any time at all during the night?"

"No." Fourth lie. How to wake up when I never slept all night long.

"So, if the defendant had left you in the middle of the night, let's say between 2.00 a.m. and 3.00 a.m., which is the approximate time of death given by the coroner, would you have known?"

"No. I wouldn't." Fifth lie.

"Your testimony is that the defendant could have gone out of the room, committed the murder, and come back to bed, and you would never have known?"

I look at her innocently. "I suppose he could have... if he'd climbed out of the window."

Something happens in her eyes. Suddenly, she realizes I'm not going to play ball, but she is stuck. She has no choice but to ask the next question.

"Why couldn't he have gone out of the door?" she asks, an odd inflection in her voice.

"Well, we were staying in an old-fashioned hotel which didn't have any surveillance so I was a bit worried about security. I locked the door and put the key inside my pillowcase."

She swallows hard. "I see. Right. Well then, he could have climbed out of the window."

"Yes, he could have done that if he had brought some ropes and climbing equipment."

The packed courtroom buzzes with interest.

"Ropes and climbing equipment?" she asks bitterly.

"Yes, our room faced a sheer cliff of a hundred feet plus that dropped into the sea."

She makes a small jerking movement with her head. She knows she's beat. There is no more to say.

I have just given Konstantin, the perfect alibi.

RAINE

https://www.youtube.com/watch?v=kOYcbod5Jow
Lost But Won

As I walk down the impressive corridor of the courthouse I see Konstantin walking towards me. We stop about six feet apart.

"You're the best thing that ever happened to me," he mouths.

"My sister showed me a video once. It was about a dog. Its master had just returned from Iraq after two years. At first the dog put its tail between its legs and ran away. Then it came back and when it was a few feet away it did the same thing again. Eventually, it came back and jumped all over the man. You should have seen it. It went crazy. The funny thing is, my sister said the reason the dog did that is because at first it didn't recognize the man. But I knew what she didn't. The dog didn't run away because it didn't recognize its owner. It ran away because it couldn't believe its own eyes. It couldn't believe it's owner had come back to it. It was too frightened that maybe it was not real. So it kept on running back. To a human that is like pinching yourself to make sure you are not dreaming." I stop and take a deep breath. "It's the same reason why I'm standing here."

"Come here," he says.

And I almost jump six feet between us into his arms. I sob like a child. "I'm yours," I say again and again.

"I know. I know. I'm so sorry, but there was no other way," he whispers in my hair.

"What do you mean?" I ask.

"Do you really think I would have held it against you when all you did was do everything in your power to save your sister?"

I look up at him, amazed. "What do you mean?"

"Oh, Raine. It was the hardest thing I've ever done in my life to pretend to cut you off and pretend I'm so shallow and horrible I would punish you by withholding treatment from Maddy. I had no choice. I had to let the enemy think I had walked away from you. Lull them into thinking they could use you as their pawn. Maddy was never in any danger. The letter you wrote to Lana only served to make me love you even more. No one is going to pay for her treatment. Only me."

Tears run down my cheeks. "I didn't know what else to do. I had to save her. It was my fault."

He kisses my cheeks. "No, it is not your fault. Nothing is your fault. You did the best you could but you were brilliant and

I'm so proud of you. You showed her the way I never could have ever imagined. You out-tricked the witch herself."

A young man clears his throat next to us.

Both of us turn towards him.

"This is for you, Mr. Tsarnov," he says, handing him an envelope.

Konstantin takes the envelope and I separate from him. He tears it open and there is a small card inside. The writing is in gold leaf. He looks at it, then he smiles.

"What is it?" I ask.

He shows me the card. I read it.

When the rat is bitten by a snake it keeps running because it thinks it escaped from the jaws of death. It doesn't know the poison is already in its veins. That it is already dead.

"Is this from Helena?" I ask.

"Maybe. It is from them anyway."

"Why are you smiling?"

"Because love will defeat them all. Every single time. They don't know it yet. All they know is the power of venom. They don't know that pure love is anti-venom."

"Come on, let's go home."

"So you never meant to leave me?"

"Of course not. It is why I told you to bring your phone to our meeting. I wanted them to hear me reject you. I wanted them to think you had no value to me. That way you do not become leverage."

"Konstantin, I have to tell you something."

"What?"

"I love you."

"You keep fucking stealing my lines."

I gaze at him in wonder. "Did you just..."

He catches my face. "Yes, I just."

"Say it."

"I love you, Miss Raine Fillander. I fucking love you. I love you so much I wanted to punch that idiot who was flirting with you."

"What idiot?"

"Yuri."

"Ah, the guy who lives in Monaco."

"That bastard is just a scammer. You don't want to know him."

"I do believe you're jealous."

"Jealous? Of course, I'm fucking jealous. I'm going out of my mind with jealousy."

I laugh, then I remember my little secret. "Konstantin, I've got something to tell you."

"What?"

I spend hours playing and replaying all the different ways I could tell him, but in the end what comes out of my mouth are the words that have been uttered by women from time immemorial.

"I'm pregnant."

KONSTANTIN

https://www.youtube.com/watch?v=y2zeudxXjuU
Right Here Waiting

"Yes, I know," I tell her.

"How?" she asks, her eyes popping.

"Because you told Lois while she had a phone on her."

"What? Were you listening to everything I said."

"Someone on our side was. We had to know what the enemy knew."

"Right. So are you... er... happy about it?"

"Happy? I was so fucking happy I broke down and cried when I read the transcript."

Her big beautiful mouth stretches into the biggest grin known to mankind.

"I knew I couldn't phone Lana Barrington so I wrote to her to plead with her to loan me some money to pay for Maddy's procedure and start to secretly arrange it so it can be carried out right after I testify. I know it was really presumptuous of me to ask after only meeting her once, but I could tell she was kind hearted and your friend, and I was really, really desperate."

"Yes, I know. She told me. Small change of plan with that one though," I tell her.

She frowns. "Change of plan?"

"You can't be the donor, Raine. You're pregnant. I don't want you to put your body through the stress that being a donor will bring. It is enough that you are trying to grow a child in your body."

Her shoulders slump, but she doesn't disagree.

"I know you really wanted to do it, but I think you've done enough for your sister, and everything is arranged. She will be admitted into hospital tomorrow"

"Tomorrow," she says with a big sigh of relief.

"Yes, tomorrow," I confirm. "Come on, let's get out of this corridor and go home."

"Home?" she whispers the word, as if she dare not say it out aloud. As if it is too precious an idea to even say aloud in case she hexes it.

I put my hand on the small of her back and led her towards the steps of the courthouse. "Yes, home. I'm moving you into my place."

She shakes her head slowly, her eyes full of love. "Not yet, my darling. I can't move in with you yet. I won't leave Mom and Maddy to fend for themselves right now. I can't donate bone marrow for Maddy, but I want to be there with her."

"Well, it'll be easier for you to do that from our place, since they'll be moving to an apartment two floors down from us."

Her eyes narrow with confusion. "What do you mean?"

"I bought an apartment two floors down from us for them."

She whirls out of the circle of my arms and stares at me with her enormous eyes. "You bought an apartment for my mom and sister?"

"Yup."

She swallows hard. "Are you kidding me?"

"No."

"That's... that's... I don't even know what to say. Than—" Her voice breaks and tears fill her eyes.

"And it's in your mother's name so even if I die tomorrow she has no worries about being homeless."

"Are you even real?" she mumbles through her tears.

"I'm real, Raine. I'm as real as the little life growing inside you. We're a family now. The three of us. And families live together."

"How can you be so sure? What if you are not acquitted?"

I grin. "You want the honest truth? We didn't even know you were going to come up with your surprise superstar performance today. We weren't counting on anything from you, as we have figured out how the murder was committed."

"You know who did it?"

"No, but we figured out how the killer did it."

"How?"

"Remember how our bed creaked."

She giggles. "How could I forget?"

"That's because they had legs. Which means there was space under it. Whoever killed Vassily didn't come in through the window. It was tightly shut from the inside. The killer arrived at least a day earlier and must have found out which room Vassily was booked into. He easily picked the old-fashioned lock of the room, once inside, all he had to do was wait. Our investigators found biscuit crumbs and other bits of food under the bed. Clearly, his mission was to steal Vassily's files, then kill him, but I met Vassily in the reception upon his arrival, he passed his files to me, and we went up to his room together."

She shivers. "So the whole time you were in the room with Vassily, the killer was under the bed."

"It is the most likely explanation."

"My God you could have been killed too!"

"I was never the target."

"I thank the universe you were not."

I take her hand and we walk down the steps together. The sun is shining brightly and I feel on top of the world. There is only one thing I haven't done yet...

RAINE

https://www.youtube.com/watch?v=N8QmRL4jDTg
It's All Coming Back To Me Now

As soon as we arrive at his, well, our home, we put our phones away into the Faraday cage, and I turn to him. "You know that time you asked me to come to that apartment... why?"

"Because I was going fucking mad being away from you. I wanted to touch you, fuck you, taste you. It was the only way I could have you for those few minutes without letting them know I still wanted you."

"Do you still have that apartment?"

"I rented it for the minimum time possible. Six months. Why?"

"Because one of these days I want to do that again. I want to arrive and have you do exactly what you did that last time."

He laughs. "You liked that, huh?"

I nod. "Yes, it was mysterious and exciting and I waited and waited for you to call me again."

"Oh, baby," he growls, as he pulls me up to him, my body pressed tightly against his as he searches my face hungrily, but for what he is looking for I can't tell. It just seems as though he can't quite believe that I belong to him. He crushes his lips to mine in a searing kiss.

I'm instantly light headed. It barely registers as he pushes the skirt of my suit up and tears off my underwear. Then he lifts me into his arms and carries me up to his bedroom. He puts me down on the ground and lays down on the bed. Then he pulls me to him and positions me until my ass is directly above his face. I gasp as he sits me down on his mouth.

Every fiber of my being feels like it is on fire.

I grind my sex wildly into his mouth as he sucks, licks and fucks me with that naughty, energetic, greedy tongue of his.

The edge of his teeth grazes and nips at the engorged bud of my clit constantly. I don't want to climax yet. I want to make it last, but it is too good. Too amazing. I rock my hips to the maddening burst of ecstasy through my body until I am completely sated.

"Now, I want you to get naked and ride me."

I love the sound of those words, the incredibly seductive tone in which he speaks them is beyond exciting.

I pull myself down his body until my ass sits on his crotch, and pull my clothes off my body. His eyes never leave my body. He leans forward and squeezing both my breasts together sucks both nipples into his warm, wet, velvety mouth. I watch him in wonder. This is my man. Mine. It seems too incredible to believe, but he is.

My breasts start to throb with pleasure. By the time my nipples pop out of his mouth they are swollen and tingling.

He looks up and our eyes meet, my heart feels as if it would burst with happiness.

"Now. Do it now," he says.

I grab his cock to position it at my entrance. We are both slick and ready, so when I take him inside me the entrance is a smooth and flawless glide.

"Ah," I whimper, as my sex sheaths his hard cock like a second skin.

I run my hand across his chest, my eyes clench shut as my body tries to adjust again to his size. Already, my sex has forgotten how big he is. Hell, he is buried so deeply inside of me I feel his thick hardness filling me all the way to my abdomen.

He lifts his upper body off the mattress, and the shift sends a sharp burst of pleasure tearing through me. He pulls his shirt over his head and his smooth, flawless skin, carved into the ridges of his torso is fully on display. I lean forward to cover his nipple with my mouth knowing it will drive him crazy. He has very sensitive nipples. When his hand comes up involuntarily to cover the hardened little buds, I seize his wrists with a laugh, and weld them to the bed on either side of him.

"Konstantin," I warn.

He gives me a heart wrenching look.

I lean forward and suck him again. He groans with pleasure.

I move my mouth upwards for a deep kiss. I suck his tongue mindlessly. Oh, how I missed this. Then I shower more kisses down his jaw. I nibble on his chin, deliberately let the tips of my breasts graze against his chest, and suck on the skin just above the frantically beating pulse in his neck. I move my lips to his neck, and down to his chest, licking, tasting, sucking, and grating my teeth across his supple flesh.

All the while my hips are rocking on him, in a slow, beguiling rhythm. Every time we are joined together like this, I'm all the more awed by him. It feels as though I've been completely transported off the earth, and thrown into another dimension where I'm not whole without him inside me.

With my knees planted firmly on the mattress, I writhe against him, guiding his cock in a to and fro motion inside of me. I do it until I can see the muscles bulging in his neck with tension.

Finally, I'm ready to fuck him properly.

With my hand planted solidly on his chest, I lift my ass off his crotch, the friction of his cock grating against my walls. It's all too sweet to process. My vision blurs and all of my focus zeroes in on the place where we are joined.

I stop just as the head is about to pop out of me. His cock completely coated with my slickness. I do a little shimmy with my hips. A sensual circle that makes his mouth open in a silent gasp. I slide back down on him.

The next time I pull my sex up him, I come back down with a vicious slam.

"Holy fuck," he pants, "Raine."

My head and heart swells with smothering heat. I think I'm going to climax. My gaze feels narrow and fuzzy. I force myself to think of something else. But my mind is blank. Fuck it. If I climax, I climax. I deserve it for today's performance in court.

I begin to ride him ruthlessly, lifting my hips and pumping back down his raging cock. My hips move with the fluidity of a snake, gyrating, grinding against him.

I thought I would climax before him, but instead I watch him come apart before me, and it's beautiful. I see him, the man who is always in control, lose control. His head thrashing from side to side.

While watching him I feel myself start to shatter, my walls contracting violently as my orgasm sears through me like a bullet. I break into pieces, every piece exploding with delicious sensations. I scream, not caring if the housekeeper hears me. This is the only way I believe I will be able to hold onto my sanity.

He pulls me down and covers my mouth with his, muffling my cries. He hooks my tongue into his mouth and sucks it hard, and it triggers my orgasm even more.

My clit throbs painfully as hot pleasure pours down my thighs, whilst I continue to writhe my hips against him, prolonging the euphoria even longer.

Eventually, when it is all over, he pulls me to him, and buries his face in my neck.

"You're a fucking miracle to me," he whispers. "You have no idea."

I fall back onto him in complete exhaustion, his cock still buried inside me.

I must have fallen asleep on his chest. I wake up with the sensation of being sticky between my legs and something very hard and hot between my pussy lips. I lift my head and he smiles at me.

"Put me back inside you," he says.

So I do and we make love again. Afterwards, we shower together. Then he makes me sit on the bed, his expression serious.

"What is it?" I ask.

"Raine, we Russians when we find something good we always like to seal the deal. I want to make you mine, permanently. Will you marry me?"

My heart feels as if it has stopped. "Yes. Of course, I'll freaking marry you."

RAINE

https://www.youtube.com/watch?v=Pl-ezoN8p_Y.
Sound Of Freedom

"I just need to run an errand for Konstantin. Will you come with me, Mom?" I say to my mom after she has helped me to move into Konstantin's place.

"Well, as long as it is not for long. I need to be back at work in three hours."

"No, it won't take long. It's just a few floors down from here."

"All right."

We take the elevator down three floors and get out. Mom says nothing as I put the key through the door and walk in. "I just have to do something in the kitchen. Have a look around."

"I'm not going to look around someone else's house."

"She won't mind. She's a really cool person. Go ahead. Have a little look. See if you like the way she has done up the place."

"Well, all right." Mom wanders off towards the living room.

I wait awhile and follow her. "Do you like it?"

"It's beautiful."

"Come and see the bedroom."

Mom follows me silently down the mirrored corridor. "Wow, look at that view. Must be nice to live here and wake up to this."

"Would you like to?" I ask quietly.

She turns towards me. "No honey. I wouldn't like to live here. The rent will be astronomical and I don't want you to be beholden to Konstantin."

"Mom, I have something to tell you."

Her jaw drops. "What?"

"Konstantin bought this apartment for you. He bought it for you and Maddy."

My mom blinks. "What?"

"He bought it for you and Maddy so we can all be close by."

She walks over to the big bed and sits on it. "This place is mine?"

I press the key into her palm. "Yes, Mom. It's all yours. Bought and paid for."

She looks up at me. "I don't know what to say. It's too much. Who will clean this big place? I could never afford to pay the yearly upkeep fees. It must be astronomical."

I kneel next to her. "Mom, you don't ever have to use that word again, astronomical. He put some money into a fund for you. He says he doesn't want you to ever have to stock shelves again. You've worked enough for three lifetimes. It's time to relax. You're going to be a lady of leisure now. Once Maddy is well again, you'll go shopping, you'll go to lunch with your friends, you'll go to the cinema, and you'll vacation in far-flung exotic countries."

My mother brushes her hand against the silky duvet on the bed. "This is my bedroom?"

"Take whichever one you want. There are three bedrooms, but this is the one with the best view."

"Maddy can have her own bedroom?"

I smile. "Yes, Maddy can have her own."

She shakes her head. "I still remember that night you found me crying in the bathroom. To think I tried to stop you from going to that auction."

"Well, we have Maddy to thank. If she had not needed the medical attention, I would never have even thought of doing something like that."

My mother squeezes my hand. "When your father left this world, I didn't know how I would manage. How I would bring up two girls on my own, but life has been good to me. You've both turned out to be little angels. I couldn't have asked for better."

I want to cry. It takes a very special person to suffer as much as my mom has and still say life has been good to her. At that moment I promise myself to turn my mother's life into a life extraordinaire.

"I love you, Mom."

She hugs me tightly. "I love you too, honey. I really, really love you. Now, if Maddy's procedure is successful, my life would be perfect."

*T*hree days later my mother's life is officially declared perfect. Maddy's transplant is successful. She claims to feel no pain at all. Later that evening Mom comes to our apartment and we open a bottle of champagne. We raise our glasses and I make a toast.

"Because life is perfect."

And we take one little sip. Afterwards we laugh, and eat, and talk until it is late. Then Mom goes down to her apartment and Konstantin and I fall into bed. We stare into each other's eyes.

"It's not a dream, is it?" I whisper.

"No my darling, it's not a dream," he whispers back. "It will be a dream when we beat the enemy, and give our children back the earth they deserve."

EPILOGUE

Raine

https://www.youtube.com/watch?v=Y0pdQU87dc8
Everything I Do I Do For You.

Konstantin is acquitted of all charges and his reputation is restored, which I expected, of course. What I didn't expect is how all his friends and business acquaintances stood by him and never once doubted his Innocence. I guess they knew, as I did, that he is good guy, incapable of such a brutal act.

It is a good day for us. We spend it in bed with a massive tub of ice cream. Sex and ice cream. I don't know if I would recommend it. It's good while it's going on, but the state of the sheets. Ugh what a mess.

Then the next day Mom and I begin to plan for the wedding. We plan it so it takes place a week after Maddy comes home from hospital. That day falls on the first week of September.

I wake up with excitement fizzing through my veins like a newly opened bottle of champagne. I sneak out of the bed I shared with Maddy that night, go to the fridge, and sit alone at my mother's kitchen island drinking some lovely, cold milk and smile to myself. I know for sure, I'm the happiest woman in the world at that moment in time.

Every dream I ever had has been fulfilled.

I'm still not showing and can just about get into my fabulous mermaid wedding dress. Mom cries when she sees me, even Maddy gets all emotional.

"The billionaire is a lucky guy," she sniffs.

Outside we couldn't have hoped for better weather. The sky is a brilliant blue and not a cloud in sight, the perfect omen. The ceremony is held in a beautiful old Russian church. It is filled with the scent of flowers. The pews are full of people, most of them I do not know. Friends and business associates of Konstantin. He has no family. He was an orphan.

None of the members of the alliance turn up. They have an understanding. They do not congregate in groups of more than two. In this way they can be taken out easily.

Maddy teases me just before I walk down the aisle. I remember feeling really nervous. My stomach in tight knots. My uncle from my father's side walks up to me. He will be giving me away.

"You look beautiful," he says. "Your dad would have been proud."

Then the music starts and I slip my hand through his elbow. We begin the walk down. I start to feel faint, like I'm floating. Then I see the most beautiful, precious man in the whole world waiting for me, his eyes, his eyes, so full of love. My heart beats so fast I think I might expire with joy.

It is a beautiful and simple ceremony, but it all goes too fast.

The reception is quite a lavish affair held at an exclusive hotel.

It's all a blur now but I remember his eyes watching me, so much love in them. I remember rice raining down on us. I remember the tall cake. I remember Maddy laughing. I remember Mom crying, I remember Lois laughing at something.

And then I remember leaving our reception and Konstantin's strong arm around my waist as we ran towards the car.

We honeymoon at the beautiful island of the Seychelles. Ah, what a happy time. We are indescribably happy. I almost dread coming back to the States. Coming back would mean facing up to all the problems, and sure enough our return is hard for me.

Konstantin would lock himself in his coding room for hours at a time while he slowly built his alternative internet, one string of zeros and ones at a time, all in his mind. And all that time I would sit around and start to worry about what would happen if the alliance doesn't win. I keep thinking of Helena's cautionary tale of the rat with the venom in his body. Running, thinking it's wounded but it has escaped, but in fact, it is already more dead than alive.

The more I think and imagine scenarios in my head, the more convinced I become that the cabal will win. To the extent, I become paranoid about it. Sometimes I will lie awake after Konstantin is sleeping. I'll listen to his deep even breathing, put my hand on my belly, and be afraid for the future.

Until one day I can bear it no more and I confront him while we are sitting together outside on the terrace. There is a full moon and it's a beautiful night, but my mind is chaotic with ugly thoughts.

"What happens if they force us all to take the chip, or the injection, or whatever it is that will turn us into AI integrated cyborgs?"

He shakes his head firmly. "They won't do that."

"Why not? If they are as evil as you say, what's to stop them?"

"Because Blake was once one of them, before he met Lana, and turned away from that life. So he knows how they think, how they operate, and what rules they are bound by. And they are very firmly bound by the rules of their religion."

He makes air quotes around the word religion.

"Even though it may seem to us as if transhumanism is merely an exercise in turning humanity into slaves or batteries that they can use to mine for energy, there is an unseen but very important spiritual element to all of it. Just like the Aztec's tore out still beating hearts and sacrificed them to their serpent God, these people believe they are harvesting souls for their God. But they can only harvest willing souls. Their rules say they are allowed to trick someone into saying yes, or make them so fearful that they say yes, but they must agree to their own enslavement."

I frown. "How can they trick us into accepting something so horrendous? Who's going to fall for something like that?"

"The same way they tricked you into agreeing to go to war with Iraq based on a lie about WMDs. Because you allowed them to fill your with unthinking fear, and because you didn't care enough to do your own research, you blindly believed the propaganda and gave your power to them. As long as humankind is not vigilant, they will tricked into giving their consent. Once they have that they can harvest your soul with no repercussions."

"Okay," I say slowly. "I get it. Like Dracula. You have to invite him in or he cannot enter your home."

"Exactly."

I take a deep breath. "It seems so impossible though, that governments, the media, and other international bodies that have been set up to protect humankind have been so captured by these ghouls."

"No, it is not as impossible as you think. Thorne once told me that he'd used his AI to map all the blue-chip companies in the world. And what he found was that no matter what industry, be it oil, pharmaceutical, food, air transport, weapons, utilities, tech, or media the majority shares of those firms are held by about ten different companies. The shares of those ten companies are mostly held by five or so companies. And the shares of those five entities are mainly owned by two companies, Blackrock and Vanguard. Then he found out the really interesting nugget of info. The biggest holder of Blackrock is Vanguard. And who owns Vanguard? We will never know, because it is privately held. Do you understand now how concentrated wealth is in our world? They own everything and everyone in power is beholden to them."

I scoot closer to him, because I feel fear in my heart for my unborn child, and I don't want to feel that. "If they own everything, how can we possibly win?"

"They want us to think there's no use fighting. They want us to give up in defeat, but the outcome is not set in stone. We are born with freedom in our bones, and that is our divine right. In this war against tyranny we have three things in our favor. First, we are many and they are few. Second, we do not extract from them, they extract from us, so they need us more than we need them. Third, they are secretly terrified of us, because they exist in a strict hierarchy of order and control, and we stand for freewill and freedom for all of humanity."

Feeling slightly more reassured, I nod. "Okay. What would be the worst-case scenario? Will we end up with a two-tier society?"

He looks sad, really sad. "If humanity doesn't come together as one and fight as one, it won't be two classes of people anymore. We will split into species. Two entirely different species."

He holds me tightly and gazes deep into my eyes. His eyes are full of sincerity. "But they won't win, Raine. I know, just as I know without any doubt in my body that our child will never be anyone's slave. Yes, they will harvest the souls of those who are not vigilant, but they won't get us, or all the people we are slowly reaching. Day by day more and more people are joining us. It is like a flame that is being passed from one heart to another. Every heart we reach, then goes out into the world, and finds more hearts to light up. That is why they are have doubled their efforts. At a certain point, the tipping point will be reached, and it will be too late for then them to do reach their goals... and we will win."

That is the last time I doubt Konstantin. I know now, that our strength is quiet, but vast. I remember and take heart from the fact that with all the power and money in the world, Helena didn't beat me. I beat her.

A New Beginning

https://www.youtube.com/watch?v=fCZVL_8Do48

*T*he promised sailing trip in the Mediterranean that Konstantin offered to take me on happens when I am nine months pregnant. We sail around the beautiful islands stopping off for long glorious lunches and romantic strolls on the beach.

It is a dreamy time. Sometimes I wake up and still half-asleep think, I'm in my little room in New York, and it was all a dream.

My baby is born on the yacht on the international seas. He belongs to no country. No one will prick the delicate skin on his tiny little heel to steal a drop of his blood so he can be put into a genetic database somewhere. I bring my son into this world to the sound of waves and water and the love I feel flowing from Konstantin's grip on my hand. It must be my child-bearing hips, but the birth doesn't last more than two hours and is not too difficult.

When the midwife leaves the room, we gaze in wonder at the new life, we have created. I remember then what Konstantin once told me. The cabal are afraid of mothers. They always have been. It has always been their terrible fear that it is the pure love of mothers that will eventually defeat them. Gazing at my newborn son wrinkled, red face, I know now, why they fear mothers. And they are right too. We will their undoing.

"He's so beautiful," I whisper.

"Yes, he is, but should he be so red?"

I laugh. "You try getting pushed out of someone's birth canal and see how red you get."

He looks sheepish. "He's actually perfect."

"He is. Look at his toes. How totally perfect they are. Like two rows of corn."

At that moment our little baby opens his eyes and looks at us both, his eyes are slightly unfocused, but still so sharp for a newborn.

"I can tell he's going to be as smart as his dad," I say with satisfaction.

"We're gonna win this war, my boy," Konstantin tells him. "We're gonna win. No matter what it takes, you *will* have a good life as a human being."

"I love you so much," I whisper looking at Konstantin.

He meets my gaze, and his eyes are shining with love. "I love you too, Raine Tsarnov. I love you more than you can ever imagine."

And it's Never Going To Be Over for them...

Want to read more of:

Blake & Lana's romance:
The Billionaire Banker

Thorne Blackborne's story:
Blackmailed By The Beast

Rocca and Autumn:
The Other Side Of Midnight

THE BILLIONAIRE BANKER

Chapter 1
Blake Law Barrington

I drop a cube of sugar into the creamy face of my espresso, stir it, and glance at my platinum Greubel Forsey Tourbillion, acquired at Christie's Important Watches auction last autumn for a cool half a million dollars.

Eight minutes past eight.

I have a party to go to tonight, but I'm giving it a miss. It's been a long day, I am tired, I have to be in New York early tomorrow morning, and it will be one of those incomprehensibly dreary affairs. I take a sip—superb coffee—and return the tiny cup to its white rim.

Summoning a waiter for the check, I sense the activity level in the room take a sudden hike. Automatically, I lift my eyes to where all the other eyes, mostly male and devouring, have veered to. Of course. A girl. In a cheap, orange dress and lap dancer's six-inch high plastic platforms.

You're looking for love in all the wrong places, honey.

A waiter in a burgundy waistcoat bearing the bill has silently materialized at my side. Not taking my eyes off the girl—despite the impossible shoes she has a good walk, sexy—I order myself a whiskey. The waiter slinks away after a right-away-sir nod, and I lean back into the plush chair to watch the show.

It is one of those swanky restaurants where there are transparent black voile curtains hung between the tables and discreet fans to tease and agitate the gauzy material. Three curtains away she stands, minus the shoes, perhaps five feet five or six inches tall. She has the same body type as Lady Gaga, girlishly narrow with fine delicate limbs. Her skin is the color of thick cream. Beautiful mouth. My eyes travel from the waist-length curtain of jet-black hair to the swelling curve of her breasts and hips, and down her shapely legs.

Very nice, but...

At twenty-nine, I am already jaded. Though I watch her with the same speculation of all the other men in the room she is a toy that no longer holds any real excitement for me. I do not need to meet her to *know* her. I have had hundreds like her—hot, greedy pussies and cold, cold hearts. It is always the same. Each one hiding talons of steely ambition that hook into my flesh minutes after they rise like resurrected phoenixes from a night in my bed. Safe to say I have realized the error of my ways.

Still....

Something about her *has* aroused my attention.

She comes further into the room and even the billowing layers of curtains cannot conceal her great beauty or youth. Certainly, she is far too young for her dining companion who has just barged in with all the grace of a retired rugby player. I recognize his swollen head instantly. Rupert Lothian. An over-privileged, nerve gratingly colossal ass. He is one of the bank's high profile private customers. The bank never does business with anyone they do not check out first and his report was sickening.

Curious. What could someone so fresh-faced and beautiful be doing with one so noted for ugly games? And they are ugly games that Lothian plays.

I watch three waiters head off towards them and the fluid, elegantly choreographed dance they perform to seat and hand them their menus. Now I have her only in profile. She has put the menu on the table and is sitting ramrod-straight with her hands tightly clasped in her lap. She crosses and uncrosses her legs nervously.

Unbidden, an image pops into my head. It is as alive and wicked as only an image can be. Those long, fine legs entangled in silky sheets. I stare helplessly as she pulls away the sheets, turns that fabulous mouth into a red O, and deliberately opens her legs to expose her sex to me. I see it clearly. A juicy, swollen fruit that my tongue wants to explore! I sit forward abruptly.

Fuck.

I thought I had passed the season of fantasizing about having sex with strangers. I reach for my whiskey and shoot it. From the corner of my eyes I see a waiter discreetly whisper something to Lothian. He rises with all the pomposity he can muster and leaves with the waiter.

I transfer my attention to the girl again. She has collapsed backwards into the chair. Her shoulders sag and her relief is obvious. She stares moodily at the tablecloth, fiddles with her purse and frowns. Then, she seems to visibly force herself away from whatever thoughts troubled her, and lets her glance wander idly around the room until her truly spectacular eyes—I have never seen anything like them before—collide with my unwavering stare. And through the gently shifting black gauze my breath is suddenly punched out of my body, and I am seized by an unthinking, irresistible call to hunt. To possess.

To *own* her.

Chapter 2
Lana Bloom

It can have been only seconds, but it seems like ages that I am held locked and hypnotized by the stranger's insolent eyes. When I recall it later I will remember how startlingly white his shirt had been against his tanned throat, and swear that even the air between us had shimmered. Strange too how all the background sounds of cutlery, voices and laughter had faded into nothing. It was as if I had wandered into a strange and compelling universe where there was no one else but me and that devilishly handsome man.

But in this universe I am prey.

The powerful spell is broken when he raises his glass in an ironic salute. Hurriedly, I tear my gaze away, but my thin façade of poise is completely shattered. Hot blood is rushing up into my neck and cheeks; and my heart is racing like a mad thing.

What the hell just happened?

I can still feel his gaze like a burning tingle on my skin. To hide, I bend my head and let my hair fall forward. But the desire to dare another look is so immense it shocks me. I have never experienced such an instant and physical attraction before.

With broad shoulders, a deep tan, smoldering eyes, a strong jaw, and straight-out-of-bed, vogue-cool, catwalk hair that flops onto his forehead, he looks like one of those totally hot and brooding Abercrombie and Fitch models, only more savage and fierce.

Devastatingly more.

But I am not here to flirt with drop dead gorgeous strangers, or to find a man for myself. I press my fingers against my flaming cheeks, and force myself to calm down. All my concentration must go into getting Rupert to agree to my proposal. He is my last hope.

My only hope.

Nothing could ever be more important than my reason for being there with such a man as him. I look miserably towards the tall doors where he has gone. This cold, pillared place of opulence is where rich people come to eat. A waiter wearing white gloves comes through the doors bearing a covered tray. I feel out of my depth. The orange dress is itchy and prickly and I long to scratch several places on my body. Then there are the butterflies flapping dementedly inside my stomach.

Don't ruin this, I tell myself angrily. You've come this far. Nervously, to regain my composure, I press my lips together and firmly push the sarcastically curving mouth out of my mind. I must concentrate on the horrible task ahead. But those insolent eyes, they will not go. So I bring to mind my mother's thin, sad face, and suddenly the stranger's eyes are magically gone. I straighten my back. Prepare myself.

I will not fail.

Rupert, having met whomever he had gone to meet, is weaving his way back to me and when our eyes touch I flash him a brilliant smile. I will not fail. He smiles back triumphantly, and coming around to my side drops me a quick kiss, before slumping heavily into his seat. I have to stop myself from reaching up to wipe my mouth.

I stare at him. He seems transformed. Expansive, almost jolly.

'That's one deal that came in the nick of time. As if the heavens have decided that I deserve you.' The way he says it almost makes me flinch with horror.

'Lucky me,' I say softly, flirtatiously, surprising myself. I tell myself I am playing a part. One that I can vanish into and emerge from unscathed, but I know it is not true. There will be repercussions and consequences.

He smiles nastily. He knows I do not fancy him, but that is part of the thrill. Taking what does not want to be taken.

'Well then,' he says. 'Don't be coy, let's hear it. How much are you going to cost me?'

I take a deep breath. A bull this large can only be taken by the horns. 'Fifty thousand pounds.'

His dirty blond eyebrows shoot upwards, but his voice is mild. 'Not exactly cheap.' His lips thin. 'What do I get for my money?'

We are both startled out of our conversation by a deep, curt voice.

'Rupert.'

'Mr. Barrington,' Rupert gasps, and literally flies to his feet. 'What an unexpected pleasure,' he croons obsequiously. I drop my head with searing shame. It is the stranger. He has heard me sell myself.

'I don't believe I've had the pleasure of your companion's acquaintance,' he says. His voice is an intriguing combination of velvet and husk.

'Blake Law Barrington, Lana Bloom, Lana Bloom, Blake Law Barrington.'

I look up then, a long way up—he is definitely over six feet, maybe six two or three—to meet his stormy-gray stare. I search them for disgust, but they are carefully veiled, impenetrable pits of mystery. Perhaps, he has not heard me sell myself, after all. I begin to tremble. My body knows something I do not. He is dangerous to me in a way I cannot yet conceive.

'Hello, Lana.'

'Hi,' I reply. My voice sounds tiny. Like a child that has been told to greet an adult.

He puts his hand out, and after a perceptible hesitation, I put mine into it. His hand is large and warm, and his clasp firm and safe, but I snatch mine away as if burnt. He breaks his gaze briefly to glance at Rupert.

'There is a party tonight at Lord Jakie's,' he says before those darkly fringed eyes return to me again. Inscrutable as ever. 'Would you like to come as my guests?' It is as if he is addressing only me. It sends delicious shivers up and down my spine. Confused, by the unfamiliar sensations I tear my eyes away from him and look at Rupert.

Rupert's eyebrows are almost in his hairline. 'Lord Jakie?' he repeats. There is unconcealed delight in his face. He seems a man who has found a bottle of rare wine in his own humble cellar. 'That's terribly kind of you, Mr. Barrington. Terribly kind. Of course, we'd love to,' he accepts for both of us.

'Good. I'll leave your names at the door. See you there.' He nods at me and I register the impression that he is obsessively clean and controlled. There is no mess in this man's life. A place for everything and everything in its place. Then he is gone.

Rupert and I watch him walk away. He has the stride of a supremely confident man. Rupert turns to face me again; his face is mean and at odds to his words. 'Well, well,' he drawls, 'You must be my lucky charm.'

'Why?'

'First, I get the deal I've been after for the last year and a half, then the great man not only deigns to speak to me, but invites me to a party thrown by the crème de la crème of high society.'

'Who is he?'

'He, my dear, is the next generation of arguably the richest family in the world.'

'*The* Barringtons?' I whisper, shocked.

'He even smells of old money and establishment, doesn't he?' Rupert says, and neighs loudly at his own joke. Rupert himself smells like grated lemon peel. The citrusy scent reminds me of Fairy washing up liquid.

A waiter appears to ask what we would like to drink.

'We'll have your finest house champagne,' Rupert booms. He winks at me. 'We're celebrating.'

A bottle and ice bucket arrive with flourish. The only time I have drunk champagne is when Billie and I dressed up to the nines and presented ourselves as bride and bridesmaid to be, at the Ritz. We pretended I was about to drop forty thousand pounds into their coffers by cutting my wedding cake there. We quaffed half a bottle of champagne and a whole tray of canapés while being shown around the different function rooms. Afterwards, Billie thanked them nicely and said we would be in touch. How we had laughed on the bus journey back.

I watch as the waiter expertly extracts the cork with a quiet hiss. Another waiter in a black jacket reels off the specials for the night and asks us if we are ready to order.

Rupert looks at me. 'The beef on the bone here is very good.'

I smile weakly. 'I guess I'll just have whatever you're having.'

'I'm actually having steak tartare.'

'Then I'll have the same.'

He looks at the waiter. 'A dozen oysters to start then steak tartare and side orders of vegetables and mashed potatoes.'

'I'm not really hungry. No starter for me,' I say quickly.

When the waiter is gone, he raises his glass. 'To us.'

'To us,' I repeat softly. The words stick in my throat.

I take a small sip and taste nothing, so I put the glass on the table and look at my hands blankly. I have to find something interesting to say.

'You have very beautiful skin,' he says softly. 'It was the first thing I noticed about you. Does it...mark very easily?'

'Yes,' I admit warily.

'I knew it,' he boasts with a sniff. 'I am a connoisseur of skin. I love the taste and the touch of skin. I can already imagine the taste of yours. A skin of wine.' He eyes me greedily over the rim of his glass.

I have been trying my best not to look at the dandruff flakes that liberally dust the shoulders of his pin-striped suit, but with that last remark he has tossed his head and a flurry of motes have floated off his head and fallen onto the pristine tablecloth. My eyes have helplessly followed their progress. I look up to find him looking at me speculatively.

'What will I be getting for my money?' His voice is suddenly cold and hard.

I blink. It is all wrong. I shouldn't be here. In this dress, or shoes, sitting in front of this obscene piece of filth hiding behind his handmade shirt, gold cufflinks and plummy, upper class accent. This man degrades and offends me simply by looking at me. I wish myself somewhere else, but I am here.

All my credit cards are maxed out. Two banks have impolitely turned me down and there is nothing else to do, but be here in this dress and these slutty shoes...

My stomach in knots, I smile in what I hope is a seductive way. 'What would you like for your money?'

'Forget what I would like for the moment. What are you selling?' His eyes are spiteful in a way I cannot understand.

'Me, I guess.'

That makes him snort with cruel laughter. 'You are an extraordinarily beautiful girl, but to be honest I can get five first class supermodels right off the runway for that asking price. What makes you think you're worth that kind of money?'

I take a deep breath. Here goes. 'I'm a virgin.'

He stops laughing. A suspicious speculative look enters his pale blue eyes. 'How old are you?'

'Twenty.' Well, I will be in two months' time.

He frowns. 'And you say you're still a virgin?'

'Yes.'

'Saving yourself up for someone special, were you?' His tone is annoying.

'Does it matter?' My nails bite into my clenched fists.

His eyes glitter. 'No, I suppose not.' He pauses. 'How do I know you're not lying?'

I swallow hard. The taste of my humiliation is bitter. 'I'll undergo any medical tests you require me to.'

He laughs. 'No need. No need,' he dismisses genially. 'Blood on the sheets will be enough for me.'

The way he says blood makes my blood run cold.

'Are all orifices up for sale?'

Oh! the brutality of the man. Something dies inside me, but I keep the image of my mother in my mind, and my voice is clear and strong. 'Yes.'

'So all that is left is to renegotiate the price?'

I have to stop myself from recoiling. I know now that I have committed two out of the nine sorts of behaviors my mother has warned me are considered contemptible and base. I have expected generosity from a miser and I have revealed my need to my enemy. 'The price is not negotiable.'

His gaze sweeps meaningfully to my champagne glass. 'Shall we give this party a go first and bargain later, when you are in a...better mood?'

I understand his thinking. He thinks he can drive the price down when I am drunk. 'The price is not negotiable,' I say firmly. 'And will have to be paid up front.'

He smiles smarmily. 'I'm sure we'll come to some agreement that we will both be happy with.'

I frown. I have been naïve. My plan is sketchy and has no provisions for a sharp punter or price negotiations. I heard through the office grapevine where I worked as temporary secretary that my boss was one of those men who are prepared to pay ten thousand pounds a pop for his pleasure and often, but I had never imagined he would reduce me to bargaining.

While Rupert stuffs himself with cheese and biscuits I excuse myself and go to the Ladies. There is another woman standing at the mirror. She glances at me with a mixture of surprise and disgust. I wait until she leaves, then I call my mother.

'Hi, Mum.'

'Where are you, Lana?'

'I'm still at the restaurant.'

'What time will you be coming home?'

'I'll be late. I've been invited to a party.'

'A party,' my mother repeats worriedly. 'Where?'

'I don't know the address. Somewhere in London.'

'How will you get home?' A wire of panic has crept into her voice.

I sigh gently. I have almost never left my mother alone at night; consequently she is now a bundle of jittery nerves. 'I have a ride, Mum. Just don't wait up for me, OK?'

'All right. Be careful, won't you?'

'Nothing is going to happen to me.'

'Yes, yes,' she says, but she sounds distracted and unhappy.

'How are you feeling, Mum?'

'Good.'

'Goodnight, then. I'll see you in the morning.'

'Lana?'

'Yeah.'

'I love you very much.'

'Me too, Mum. Me too.'

I flip my phone shut with a snap. I no longer feel cheap or obscene, but strong and sure. There is nothing Rupert can do that can degrade me. I will have that money no matter what.

I look at myself in the mirror. No need for lipstick as I have hardly eaten—just watching Rupert gurgle down the oysters made me feel quite sick, and how was I to know steak tartare was ground raw meat. For a moment I think again of that sinfully sophisticated man, his eyes edged with experience and mystery, his lips twisted with sensuality, and I am suddenly overcome by a strong desire to press my body against his hard length. But he is gone and I am here.

I return my phone to my purse and go out to meet my fate.

Read More Here:
The Billionaire Banker

Chapter 1
Chelsea

https://www.youtube.com/watch?v=0-7IHOXkiV8&list=
RDhn3wJ1_1Zsg&index=24
"Oh, Father tell me, do we get what we deserve?"

"Ms. Appleby."

The busy street below my window suddenly ceases to exist. I freeze, not daring to even take a breath.

Thorne Blackmore?

No. No. No. It can't be. He couldn't have found me here.

And yet ... I would recognize that voice anywhere. Husky and beautiful. I hear the click of my office door closing and his footsteps come closer. Closer still. So close I can feel the heat from his body. The raw power of his energy surrounds me and makes my skin tingle. In the industry they call him The

Beast, because he is so cold and ruthless, his methods are pitiless.

"Hello, Chelsea," he whispers in my ear. The familiar rumble of his voice is bittersweet. Greedily, I drag in the scent of his aftershave, leather, pine forests, and the tangy ocean. I shut my eyes. Oh, sweet Jesus. How I have missed him. These last two years without seeing him have been hell. How did I survive? I walked wounded and bewildered. Days passed, then weeks, the leaves changed, the cold winds came, then the mornings began to fill with sunlight again. After the first year, I lied to myself. I told myself I had forgotten him. But like a ghost, this man haunted me.

Will he still match the memory I keep deep in my heart?

I take a step forward, then turn around to face him. For a second my whole body goes cold. It is like coming home to find that a leopard has leapt in through your kitchen window and it is eating your sweet little dog. He's standing there in his usual ten-thousand dollar suit and thousand dollar tie, but he is bulkier, deadlier, bloodier, scarier and; oh God, his eyes. The gray orbs were never warm before, but now they are as frozen as the most inhospitable winter lake. And yet he is *beautiful.* Beautiful like lightning ripping through the night sky, or the angry sea crashing into cliffs. The breath I was unconsciously holding escapes in a rush, and I stand there like a deer, beyond conscious control, motionless, sniffing the air, terrified, ready to run.

He studies me expressionlessly.

For a few seconds, I can do nothing but stare into those piti-less eyes. Then I force a bright, happy smile onto my face. *Pretend, Chelsea. You can do this. Just pretend.* "Hiya. What a lovely surprise to see you again." My voice sounds breathy and shaky.

He smiles slowly. A cold, mocking smile. Undertones of danger.

Oh, Mother of God. I decide to take the bull by the horns. "I know you must be angry, I'm really sorry I stole from you."

His smile grows. It could be mistaken for an almost friendly grin except for the hostile wasteland in his eyes. "Are you now?" he murmurs.

"Yes, yes, I am very, very sorry. It was a mistake. I shouldn't have done it. I'll make immediate arrangements to return the money to you."

His blunt charcoal eyelashes sweep down, and I stare at him hungrily. I never expected to see him again. He is spectacularly elusive. Even catching a glimpse of him is hard. He *is* hard. "What kind of arrangements might they be?"

"I ... I have some savings and I'll take a loan for the rest and pay it all back."

"All of it?"

"Every last cent."

"With interest?'

"Of course," I agree instantly, even though I feel my stomach tighten. I probably won't be able to afford it, but maybe I can make a deal to pay him back monthly, or something.

His eyes glitter. "And the cost of finding you? Will you pay that back too?"

"The cost of finding me?" I repeat stupidly.

"Yes, it is very, very difficult to find a girl who stops using her credit cards, social media, and completely drops off the face of the earth."

"Well, living in New York is not exactly dropping off the face of the earth."

"Let's just say it is hard to find someone when you're looking for Chelsea Appleby, and she is living under the name of Alison Mountbatten, and has gone to considerable trouble to erase her digital footprint from the net. Didn't you ever miss going to your favorite online store to get those black shoes you love so much or that peach lipstick you always wear?"

My mouth feels like it's full of dust. I swallow hard. "Well, yes. However, I figured a new life was the best way forward."

"Hmmm ..."

"Look, you can either tell me now, or let me know later how much I owe you. I'll make the arrangements straight away. But I ... er ... have a pile of work to finish right now." I wave my hand in the direction of my desk.

"Um ... I suppose we could call it two million even."

My eyes pop wide open. "What? You can't be serious! You want two million? I stol ... took $300,000."

He shrugs carelessly. "Interest ... opportunity costs."

"Interest ... opportunity costs?" I echo incredulously.

"Three hundred thousand in my hands has unlimited investment potential," he sneers.

I frown. Thorne is so freaking rich he can give away three hundred thousand dollars without batting an eyelid. This is the man who flies hand-churned butter from France to wherever he is in the world. Three hundred thousand is a drop in the ocean to him. "Why? Why are you doing this? You don't even need it. All those billions sitting in your bank account. You couldn't spend it even if you tried. You don't even care about it. They're just numbers to you."

He takes his phone out of his expensive camel coat. "It's the principle."

"It's nothing to you. It's less than the cost of a round-trip in your private plane."

He lets his eyes flick to the phone in his hand. "But if you'd rather I alert the proper authorities instead—"

Panic surges through my veins. I raise my hand up. "Wait. Just wait a second. We can work something out. I'll pay it all back. I swear. I will. I just need a bit of time."

"So you can run away." His voice is icy.

"I won't run." Taking a rasping breath, I stare into his cold, watching eyes. "I promise."

He takes a step closer and I stop breathing. His hand rises up and he runs his finger down my exposed throat. "So soft and pale," he murmurs as his thumb caresses the skin where a pulse is kicking. "How can I trust a thief and a liar?"

"I give you my word," I choke out.

He shakes his head slowly. "No, Chelsea. Your word is not good enough. It was once, but not anymore."

To my horror my eyes fill with tears. When I blink, they spill down my cheeks. He laughs. "The oldest trick in the book, Chelsea. I should have known you'd stoop to that. Well, I'm afraid female tears have the opposite effect on me." He bends his head and licks my cheek, his tongue warm and velvety. He lifts his head and meets my stunned eyes. "They excite me. You, my little thief, are going to cry for me. A lot."

I did not realize that my hands had flown up. I must have wanted to shove him away, but they are resting on his chest, my fingers spread out on the hard muscles. "What do you want from me?" I whisper hoarsely.

"I want you to pay your debt with your body."

I hear my blood rushing in my ears, and I stare at him in shock. "What do you mean?"

"For three months, you will be my toy. You will sleep when I tell you to sleep, you will eat when I tell you to eat, and when I tell you to spread your legs, your only thought will be, how wide. During that season when you will be mine, I will use you when, where, and how I decide."

"You can't do that to me," I gasp.

"Or you can go to prison. You will be very sweet meat in a women's prison. All this soft, unmarked flesh."

I shudder and he smiles. "Yes, Chelsea, shudder you should. Trust me, my cock would be infinitely better."

"You could have any woman. Why are you doing this?"

"Because I can. Now strip."

Read More Here:
Blackmailed By The Beast

Chapter 1
Autumn

It's just struck midnight, but I've no thoughts yet of leaving the backroom in the art shop where I double as Larry's shop assistant and cleaner, and going home. I sneaked back in here after dinner to work on my little painting, but I've become so totally engrossed in it, I could be here for hours more.

I know most artists prefer working in daylight. Not me. I love creating things long after everyone else is tucked up in their beds and the air is shimmering with all their dreams.

I load my brush with the precious oil paints that take up a great proportion of my wages and let it glide effortlessly across the canvass. Almost as if it has a will of its own. I'm still a student with much to learn, but I have to admit my painting is starting to look good. Exceptionally good. Maybe because this painting is special... important.

Well, at least to me, it is.

I take a few steps back to gaze critically at my canvas. It's a strange scene. An old, crumbling, ivy covered castle built into the side of a snow-capped mountain. A road, so narrow only a horse driven carriage could fit, leads up to the fortress. I'm tempted to add a carriage and snorting black horses onto the road, but I'm afraid I'll spoil the painting.

It's important I don't ruin it since I've attempted to paint this scene countless times, but always had to give up after a few strokes. I knew instinctively I can't capture the vivid image in my mind, and something deep inside me demanded I replicate it exactly as it lived in my mind. I can't understand why I had to, I just knew I did.

I start moving forward to add more color to the castle, when I freeze. The skin at the back of my neck is prickling and goose pimples are rising up on my arms. The silence is undisturbed, but the air is different.

My heart slams into my rib cage as I swing my head around and look through the half-open door into the small showroom beyond. All the lamps are turned off, but from the light of the streetlamps I can see right through to the rusty little bells attached to the door. I've been so lost in my work I've not heard them ring, but I know.

Someone has entered the shop!

It can't be a customer at this time of the night, and I know it is not Larry. He would have called out. It is either one of the wild kids in town up to no good, or a robber. Dad sent me for karate classes when I was in high school and I know some good moves. I can definitely handle any kid, and probably even a robber, if he isn't carrying a gun.

But I have an even better idea.

I reach for a stained rag on the wooden trolley next to me and hurriedly wipe off as much paint from my hands so it won't be slippery and tip toe over to the cupboard. I throw the cloth on the floor and pick up the baseball bat next to the cupboard. Gripping the smooth solid wood tightly with both hands, I start to move stealthily towards the door. I'll be damned if I'm going to be cowed by any intruder.

My heart is beating so fast, my blood roars in my ears. I'm ready to swing the bat hard at the slightest provocation... until I trip on the temporary plastic covering Larry placed over some wires he ran across the room just until the electrician came on Monday.

I've bumped my foot against the plastic a few times, but always managed to regain my balance. Not this time. This time the damn thing finally gets me. I feel myself pitch forward. My hands instinctively let go of the bat and fling out to try and grab on to anything that would break my fall, but I only connect with the trolley full of paint tubes and a jar of turpentine filled brushes.

Grasping for the trolley is a big mistake. Not only does it not stop my fall, it accelerates it. The trolley shoots a few feet forward, until it collides with an immovable object, then both the trolley and I crash to the concrete floor in an almighty racket.

The breath is knocked out of me as my back slams onto the floor and paint tubes bounce off me and the jar hits my chest and spills out its contents. I can feel the pungent turpentine seeping into my clothes and reaching my skin.

"Shit," I curse, as I lie there a winded, bruised, stained mess.

Then, I become aware there is someone else in the room with me. I turn my head and see a pair of highly polished black shoes a few feet away from me. My shocked eyes travel upwards and my brain notes how immaculate the creases in his black trousers are. The material is smooth, expensive. He is wearing a long black coat that looks luxuriously soft, the way good cashmere does.

A belt with a custom insignia on the buckle. A two-headed eagle or a phoenix perhaps.

My gaze travels further upwards. Flat stomach. Black turtle-neck sweater. Pale skin, blond hair, sensual mouth, strong jaw, narrow nose and...

Suddenly, my eyes lock with the stranger's, and something shifts inside of me.

I hold my breath without even realizing it. As I stare into those translucent icy blue irises full of mysteries. Time stops. It isn't the way romance books describe it. The rest of the world doesn't drop away. Instead those eyes reach into my soul and whirl me away into another world. It's like a sense of déjà vu as if I've once danced in the snow with this man while a full orchestra played just for us.

I think of steel hardened by fire and feel strong sexual desire for him flower in my belly, but I just can't explain why I would feel that. He is sooooo not my type. I'm contemptuous of arrogant rich men who believe they can buy anything with their money. And there is no doubt he is such a man. I can tell by the curve of his mouth. Nothing has been denied this man. Ever.

For he is like a marvelous piece of art. His pale beauty and gold hair have a strange... darkness to them that immediately makes you wary, but is at the same time so magnetic, so fascinating, you can't look away, you want in. And all you can do is stand there, or in my case, lie there and stare stupidly.

"Are you alright?" he asks. His voice has a hypnotic quality, smooth as honey dripping from a spoon, but laced with a powerful note of authority.

I want to hear him speak again.

He takes another step towards me and bends slightly from his great height to hold a hand out to me. At the moment, I realize something else about him. He is clean. Immaculately clean. Not a blonde hair out of place, not a speck of dust on his expensive clothes, his nails are beautifully manicured, and his skin is so clear and blemish free it is as if he is one of those Gods from Mount Olympus who used to occasionally step down to earth to mate with human women.

I feel my hackles rise.

I do not like this man at all.

I know wholeheartedly, instinctively, definitely.

He is dangerous to me.

Read More Here:
The Other Side Of Midnight

ABOUT THE AUTHOR

If you wish to leave a review for this book
please do so here:
The Russian Billionaire

Please click on this link to receive news of my latest releases
and great giveaways.
http://bit.ly/1oe9WdE

and remember
I **LOVE** hearing from readers so by all means come and say
hello here:

ALSO BY GEORGIA LE CARRE

His Frozen Heart

The Man In The Mirror

A Kiss Stolen

Can't Let Her Go

Highest Bidder

Saving Della Ray

Nice Day For A White Wedding

With This Ring

With This Secret

Saint & Sinner

Bodyguard Beast

Beauty & The Beast

The Other Side of Midnight

Made in the USA
Las Vegas, NV
21 June 2021

25153972R00178